FOR 83 YEARS, THE UNIQUE MAGAZINE
January-February 2006

ISSN 0898–5073
Cover by Rowena Morrell

Weird Tales® is published 6 times a year by Wildside Press, LLC in association with Terminus Publishing Co., Inc. Postmaster and others: send all changes of address and other subscription matters to Wildside Press, 9710 Traville Gateway Drive # 234, Rockville MD 20850. Single copies, $5.95 in U.S.A. & possessions; $7.00 by mail to Canada, $10.00 by first class mail elsewhere. Subscriptions: 6 issues $24.00 in U.S.A. & possessions; 33.00 in Canada, in U.S. funds. Editorial matters and single-copy orders should be addressed to *Weird Tales*®, 121 Crooked Lane, King of Prussia PA 19406–2570. Publisher is not responsible for loss of manuscripts in publisher's hands or in transit; please see page 8 for more details. Copyright © 2006 by Wildside Press, LLC. All rights reserved; reproduction prohibited without prior permission. Typeset & printed in the United States of America. *Weird Tales*® is a registered trademark owned by Weird Tales, Limited.

Cold Tonnage Books, 22 Kings Lane, Windlesham, Surrey, GU20 6JQ, United Kingdom, andy@coldtonnage.co.uk, offers subscriptions to *Weird Tales*® at £27 for six issues in the United Kingdom, £30 elsewhere, payment in sterling by cheques, money orders, or Pay Pal.

Get Your Magazines Here!

DNA Publications is proud to bring you the very best genre magazines that you can find anywhere. Check out our great magazine and save off the newsstand price. Join us as we redefine genre publishing and lead the field into the next Golden Age!

Dreams of Decadence

If vampires are what you're after, then check out *Dreams of Decadence*. Each issue features poetry and fiction by award-winning writers such as Tanith Lee, Lawrence Watt-Evans, Josepha Sherman, Brian Stableford, and Tippi N. Blevins. Subscribe today—life is too short to miss a single issue! Join us on our journey down the crimson path as we explore eternity.

Fantastic Stories

Brings you the best of it all. Now you can get the best fantasy, and science fiction stories all in one place. You'll get fiction by writers such as Allen Steele, Tom Piccirilli, David Bischoff, Ed Gorman, Esther Friesner, Jack Cady, Alan Dean Foster, Shariann Lewitt, Paul Di Filippo, Chris Bunch, and Josepha Sherman. This one is worth taking a look at!

Mythic Delirium

is the top circulation genre poetry magazine. In its pages you'll find poems from writers such as Ian Watson, Jane Yollen, Ann K. Schwader, Darrell Schweitzer, Joe Haldeman, and Ursula K. Le Guin.

Absolute Magnitude

is where the action is. We deliver one pulse pounding adventure after another, no one else even comes close. Come home to the sense of wonder that first hooked you on science fiction, with stories by writers such as Harlan Ellison, Allen Steele, Chris Bunch, Alan Dean Foster, Hal Clement, Terry Bisson, and Sharon Lee and Steve Miller.

Exciting books from DNA Publications!

For the first time in one place, DNA Publications brings you two-time Hugo Winner Allen Steele's nonfiction. This hardcover contains essays and travelogs that span Steele's entire career, taken from diverse places including the pages of magazines such as *Absolute Magnitude* and from Steele's testimony before the United States Congress. Steele shares deeply interesting insights into the future of space travel, the state of science fiction, and where both are heading. This is a must-read for any Allen Steele fan. Order today and your copy will be autographed by the author!

New from DNA Publications, best-selling author Chris Bunch's exciting Shadow Warrior Trilogy will leave you on the edge of your seats. In *The Wind After Time,* meet Joshua Wolfe, a bounty hunter and spy who must battle a host of powerful enemies in a race to save the known universe. Follow him on his search for the dreaded Al'ar in *Hunt the Heavens,* and be amazed by the trilogy's stunning conclusion in *The Darkness of God.* Bunch is a masterful storyteller, and the Shadow Warrior series shows him at his best. Also available from DNA Publications is the hardcover omnibus edition which includes all three trade volumes as well as a never-before-collected Joshua Wolfe short story. All books ordered through of this special offer will be autographed by the author!

DNA Publications is proud to bring you *Dreams of Decadence Presents #1.* Tippi N. Blevins and Wendy Rathbone have been reader favorites ever since their work first appeared in the pages of *Dreams of Decadence,* the only professional magazine specializing in poetry and fiction about vampires. In the tradition of *Dreams of Decadence* this dual collection brings you some of the best vampire-related stories and poetry that you'll find anywhere.

The *DNA Helix* brings you two stories from each of our four fiction magazines: *Weird Tales, Fantastic Stories, Dreams of Decadence,* and *Absolute Magnitude,* with stories from your favorite authors including Sharon Lee and Steve Miller, Charlee Jacob, Jamie Wild, Warren Lapine, and others. Preorder your copy today and you'll get it when it's hot off the press before it even hits the stores. This anthology is the perfect way to get a feel for all four of our fiction magazines.

The *Absolute Magnitude* Anthology is where the action is. Covering the first seven issues of *Absolute Magnitude,* you'll find many of SF's biggest stars such as Terry Bisson, Hal Clement, Chris Bunch, Allen Steele, Geoffrey A. Landis, Janet Kagan, Alan Dean Foster, and others. Order directly from us and your copy will be autographed by the editor. *Absolute Magnitude* started the DNA publications empire, check it out here!

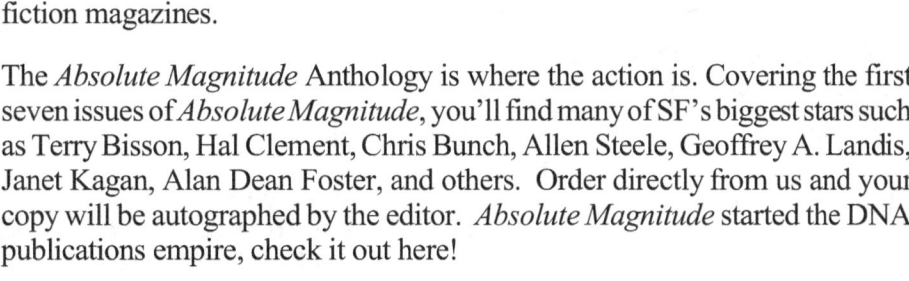

Thor's Fist takes the reader on a wild ride through an alternate universe where magic works and the gods are real.

New from Wildside Press . . .

Achmed Abdullah's name was once synonymous with adventure. He published dozens of novels and hundreds of short stories in the pulp magazines of the early 20th century, thrilling millions of readers throughout the world. He wrote with authority about exotic peoples and places because he had lived a life filled with adventure, serving in the British army and travelling extensively to exotic locales before settling down to a literary career.

Here is the first new book of Adbullah's stories in almost 70 years. "A Charmed Life" tells of one life-changing night in India, when a white man glimpses and beautiful woman in danger and acts to rescue her. "Framed at the Benefactor's Club" is a fascinating, intricately plotted mystery set in Manhattan. "The Yellow Wife" is a chilling look at life in Chinatown. "Bismallah!" is a light adventure in Africa, as crooked traders try to put a successful rival company out of business. "Light" is a surprisingly effective supernatural tale. "A Yarkand Survey" tells the story of a corrupt governor who is sent on a survey mission that might cost him his life -- if he isn't careful! And "Fear" is the tale of two thieving white men in Africa and the weird fates that awaited them.

Ranging from mystery to adventure to outright horror, from the streets of New York to the rooftops of Calcutta, from London's Chinatown to the jungles of Africa, here are tales of men caught up by plots and mysteries beyond their wildest imaginings! Features a new introduction by pulp scholar Darrell Schweitzer.

FEAR, by Achmed Abdullah

[ ] $19.95 (trade paperback)
[ ] $35.00 (hardcover)

Add $3.95 shipping in the U.S.
Other countries: see our web site
at www.wildsidepress.com

Name: _____

Address:_____

Address:_____

Mail to: Wildside Press, LLC
9710 Traville Gateway Dr. #234
Rockville, MD 20850

Looking Backwards In Several Directions At Once

Now that *Weird Tales*® is undergoing one of its periodic transitions, with a new publishing arrangement, increased page-count and frequency, and the return of John Betancourt to the editorial team, it seems like a good time to reconsider what this magazine is, what it stands for, and where it came from.

We have very deep roots. This is a magazine of *stories* and the art of storytelling is a very ancient one, probably *the* oldest profession, with all due respect to another ancient occupation. Some aspects of it do not change, even over thousands of years, because people do not change. A story is basically a narrative device for sharing emotion and experience, and also for imposing coherence onto the stuff of reality. Particularly because the stories in *Weird Tales*® so often focus on really basic things — fear, death, love, growth — what constitutes a story is pretty much constant.

Of course the *form* changes

somewhat. Twentieth-century writers played lots of tricks with form. Jorge Luis Borges wrote a story in the form of a book review, and another in the form of an encyclopedia entry. Certainly we don't tell our stories as long poetic epics, as did Homer or even John Milton. *Why* has the long narrative poem declined in past century? *Has* there been a successful "epic" since Stephen Vincent Benét's "John Brown's Body" in 1928? That is the subject of another essay. Are the poets not up to epics any longer? Is the audience not up to them?

For all that we use a lot of shorter poems (and once did run a brilliant four-page mock-epic by John M. Ford called "Troy: The Movie" in *WT* 308, well before there *was* a movie called *Troy*), the basic medium for this magazine is prose. Prose narrative consists of description and dialogue. The key to effective narration is that the writer must fully develop at least the key scenes, rather than synopsize them, so the reader can share the expe-

rience of the story rather than just "hear" about it. Students of literature have noticed that prose forms evolve over time, that the tightly-focussed short story is a nineteenth-century invention, and that a novel written in author-omniscient viewpoint with the author's voice butting in to address the "Dear Reader" and comment on the story is these days — at the very least — a bit quaint. (But, in a Post-Modern sense, it could be done with deliberate irony.)

That may be so, but if Apuleius were alive today we'd want him to write for *Weird Tales*®. It is true that he wrote in Latin (but we would use translations) and that he flourished in the third quarter of the second century A.D., making him roughly a contemporary with Marcus Aurelius; but we recommend that *Weird Tales*® readers should go look up his novel, *The Golden Ass*, and not only enjoy it, because it is a gloriously alive book, but note its affinity with what we do here in this magazine. There's a great scene early on, in which a traveler in Thessaly (which everybody *knew* was the most witch-haunted place on Earth) stops at an inn with a companion. They go to sleep in separate beds in the same room. The first traveller awakens in the middle of the night, just as levitating witches come floating in through the window, gathering like a sinister cloud over the companion's bed. One of them drifts down, slits the hapless fellow's throat with a knife, then reaches into the wound and pulls out his heart, substituting a sponge in its place. The first traveler is, of course, terrified, not merely at what is going on but at the prospect that the witches will notice that he is watching them. Of course they do. They flip over his bed, urinate on him, and fly out the window. Was it a dream? Smelling somewhat the worse for wear, and certain that no one will believe him, the traveler resolves to escape before he can be charged with murder. He slips out to the stable to saddle his horse, and is astonished to meet his companion, apparently unharmed. They travel throughout the day, but the first man cannot quite convince himself that it was all a dream. Tension mounts. They come to a stream. The companion gets down to drink, the sponge in his chest gets wet and falls out, and he dies.

This may be from eighteen and a half centuries ago, but it's *Weird Tales*® material. *The Golden Ass* is a surprisingly modern, or even Post-Modern book, full of questions about the nature of reality and the reliability of narrators. A contemporary equivalent could be passed off as "magic realism" or even "slipstream." It is also clearly the cultivated end-product of centuries of development, with its roots in the Hellenistic Age (the period between Alexander the Great and the coming of the Romans, when much of the Mediterranean area was ruled by Greek kings). It was written for an

---

STAFF:
Publisher: John Betancourt
Editors: George H. Scithers, Darrell Schweitzer, & John Betancourt
Managing Editor: Sean Wallace. Art Editor: Diane Weinstein
Assistant Editors: Robert Waters & Myke Cole
Typesetting: Owlswick Press

MANUSCRIPT SUBMISSIONS:
We will be reading unsolicited manuscripts again in March 2006 — and then, as always, by mail in standard manuscript format. To survive, all editors insist on a few Rules: each submission must be in proper format and must include a return envelope, addressed to you, with enough U.S. Postage affixed to bring the manuscript back to you. If you want us to discard the manuscript if we don't buy it, tell us so. In that case include a business-sized envelope, addressed to you, with U.S. Postage affixed, so we can send you our comments. No loose stamps, please. Before submitting your manuscript, please send us a business-sized envelope, with postage affixed, addressed to you, for our guidelines.
The address for submissions and all other editorial matters:
Weird Tales®, **121 Crooked Lane, King of Prussia PA 19406–2570**
An e-mail version of our guidelines is available for the asking from WEIRDTALES@COMCAST.NET
Visit our message board: http://www.wildsidepress.com

The address for subscriptions, subscribers' changes of address, advertising, and money matters is:
Wildside Press, 9710 Traville Gateway Drive # 234, Rockville MD 20850
Visit us on the Web at: <www.wildsidepress.com> and <www.weirdtalesmagazine.com>
We recommend two books on writing: *On Writing Science Fiction: the Editors Strike Back!* by Scithers, Schweitzer, & John M. Ford; $19.50, postpaid, in hardcovers from Owlswick Press, 121 Crooked Lane, King of Prussia PA 19406–2750. (We wrote it, so of course we speak highly of it.) In Pennsylvania, add $1.19 sales tax. The other is the always essential *The Elements of Style*, by William Strunk, Jr., & E.B. White, available from any good bookstore.

We are not responsible for manuscripts in our hands or in transit.
You must put your *name* and *address* on the first page of every manuscript. For all manuscripts:

`use 12-point type`

`on 24-point spacing, like this,` please!

Öwlswick Press

THE ADVENTURES OF DOCTOR ESZTERHAZY
by **Avram Davidson**, with full-color dust jacket by **George Barr**, interior drawings by **Todd Cameron Hamilton**, and a foreword by **Gene Wolfe**.

Analog Science Fiction & Fact wrote: "Between 1974 and 1986, Avram Davidson published a number of stories of such astonishing skill, erudition, wit, and quirkiness that major markets such as *The New Yorker* and *Playboy* wouldn't touch them with a ten-foot Bulgarian. Set on the cusp between the nineteenth and the twentieth centuries in Scythia-Pannonia-Transbalkania, the fourth largest empire in Europe (the Turks were fifth) and a literal neighbor of the comic-opera realms of Graustark and Ruritania, flavored with Gilbert & Sullivan, Twain, Chesterton, and Conan Doyle (et only Davidson knows the cetera), they starred Engelbert Eszterhazy as a gentleman in search of learning wherever he might find it, unfazed by the strangest of events, cleverly combining the data that came his way to solve mysteries and ease the lots of the polyglot peoples of the empire. . . . Buy it."

In *Newsday*, Gregory Feeley wrote: "The stories are mannered, witty, and filled with the ornate archaisms of Davidson's mature style. . . . Davidson is the peer of John Collier and Lord Dunsany, and *The Adventures of Doctor Eszterhazy* is one of his finest books."

Tom Whitmore, in *Locus, the Newspaper of the Science Fiction Field*, wrote: "But what about these stories, I hear you ask. What are they about, and why should I read them? They are about Engelbert Eszterhazy, possessor of six doctorates; they are about the empire of Scythia-Pannonia-Transbalkania and its tribulations; they are about wonder, marvel, and the unexpected.

"They are Victorian tales, with a Victorian pace, with the richness of language that makes the best Victoriana so marvelous, and with modern allusions and understanding lurking just beneath the surface; to try to summarize them individually is to wreak havoc on their integrity. There are wonders here for those who know a little, and marvels for those who know a lot, about literature, history, botany, or any other subject.

"But you should read these stories because they are fun. They amuse, instruct, alert, puzzle, and challenge in the way that only great stories can. The publisher's conceit of having each story identified by an icon rather than a running title is totally appropriate. . . . A masterful performance from both author and publisher!"

Avram Davidson wrote *The Phoenix and the Mirror, Peregrine: Primus, Peregrine: Secundus*, and *Vergil in Averno*, along with many other classics of erudite, witty fantasy.

Hardcover, 386 pages: $24.50 postpaid from Owlswick Press, 121 Crooked Lane, King of Prussia PA 19406-2570

audience capable of reading a sophisticated text rather than listening to the chanting of a tribal bard. There were many other such works which have not survived, including whole genres of fantastic fiction. (The late critic Sam Moskowitz once tried to convince us that the emperor Tiberius was a science fiction fan, due to his fondness for fantastic travel narratives.)

All this was lost in the Dark Ages and had to be re-invented, not surprisingly, from classical models. But, as the French say, the more things change, the more they stay the same. The basic requirements of storytelling do not change all that much because human emotions do not change. *The Golden Ass* is a roller coaster of ghostly and ghastly horror, comedy, beauty, and strangeness. It would make a great Terry Gilliam film.

It's a whole other essay, too, to describe where magazines came from, but that is the other thread of where *Weird Tales*® originated. Suffice it to say that the modern "magazine" began in the eighteenth century as a single, newspaper-sized sheet, which was printed on both side and distributed in English coffee houses. Much of the contents of these, *The Spectator* and others like it, were reprinted as books. They featured some fiction, mostly didactic fables, though we have four volumes of *The Adventurer* from 1770 which contain lots of "Oriental" fiction, some of it pseudo-Arabianized fairy tales.

Magazines developed steadily throughout the nineteenth century. Edgar Allan Poe wrote for many and edited some. The closest thing to

Weird Tales® prior to *Weird Tales*® itself was a reported periodical (very rare) from the early nineteenthth century that featured pirated condensations of Gothic Novels. But the real breakthrough came in 1896, when Frank Munsey turned *The Argosy* into a low-priced, all-fiction publication and thus invented the pulp magazine. This roughly where *Weird Tales* came in. Pulps soon began to specialize into magazines of western stories, detective stories, and the like. (Not to mention Northwest adventures; South Sea stories; flying stories; and, yes, there really was a *Zeppelin Stories,* although *Spicy Oriental Zeppelin Stories* remains mythical — so far.) In 1923, Joseph Henneberger decided to start a magazine devoted to horror and fantasy, the sort of periodical to which a latter-day Poe might submit his stories. (And sure enough, Henneberger soon discovered H.P. Lovecraft.) The title comes from a line in Poe's "Dream-Land": *From a wild, weird clime that lieth, sublime / Out of SPACE — out of TIME.*

So *Weird Tales*® has had a clear mission and identity from the start. We're not the first to admit that some of the early issues aren't very good, though they are fascinating; and you can now read them in facsimile editions from Girasol Collectables, which are thousands of dollars less expensive than the originals and a lot more durable. Henneberger's first editor, Edwin Baird, may not have been completely in his element with *Weird Tales*. His run ended in bankruptcy after 13 issues. He did a lot better with *Detective Tales*. It was *WT*'s

second editor, Farnsworth Wright (1924–40) who gave the magazine the magic with which it is still imbued. Wright developed (or discovered) all the *WT* greats — Lovecraft, Howard, Smith, Whitehead — except for a few late arrivals like Ray Bradbury and Fritz Leiber who appeared under the auspices of his very capable successor, Dorothy McIlwraith.

Of course the pulp era is long gone, blown away by the advent of television and the mass-market paperback book, but *Weird Tales*® persisted. The first incarnation folded in 1954 and the name lived on as a source for so many great stories reprinted from its pages. It was revived, 1973–74, again in 1980, again in 1984–85 and finally, and more permanently in 1987 by Terminus Publishing Co., Inc.. We took it as a good omen that in the same year Marvin Kaye brought out an anthology entitled, *Weird Tales: The Magazine That Never Dies.*

Argueably, the essential nature of a story hasn't changed in thousands of years, and the form of the short story has been around since the nineteenth century. Furthermore, the definition of a magazine hasn't changed all that much in hundred years or so, though how magazines are produced and distributed certainly has, the most important changes being the advent of desktop typesetting and the shift from newsstands to bookstore magazine racks, all in the last twenty years. Yet this shouldn't be taken as a recipe for stagnation. It was our unofficial slogan in the early years that our version of *Weird Tales*® was to be "a resurrec-

tion, not an exhumation." What we meant by that — and still mean — is that we don't want to publish pastiches of the great stories of seventy years ago, any more than the old pulp *Weird Tales* in its heyday, circa 1930, was devoted to a careful re-creation of the fantastic literature of 1860.

Eternal verities are all well and good, but you do have to move with the times. How? Not by going the "experimental" route, surely. In every generation certain writers, usually young ones, decide that their work is too "advanced" for such traditional elements as characterization, coherent narrative, and identifiable emotions. This never works. The readers go away, and the writers who survive are the ones who learn, however grudgingly, that they need to tell stories after all. (In science fiction this happened in the late 1960s and was called the New Wave.)

But "experimental" writing, being a literary fossil, never evolves much; and a generation later, someone tries it again.

No, the way stories change with the times is by responding to a new cultural experience. It can be something as obvious as the advent of cyberspace and the home computer. This has certainly raised new imaginative possibilities, even for stories about ghosts and magic. Kelly McCullough, Ian Watson, and others have done good work here. (We can waggishly claim that "The Grave of My Beloved," by Ian Watson and Roberto Quaglia, which we will publish soon, contains what might well be the first example of "virtual necrophilia" in literature. You'll read it here. . . .) Or, consider a classic story we

reprinted a couple issues back, "The Upper Berth" by F. Marion Crawford, originally published in the 1890s. This was very much a cutting-edge story in its day. There had of course been stories about haunted ships for a long time; and one more ghostly apparition in a rotting wooden sailing ship would have hardly been noticed; but the idea that a deadly ghost could still be found on a bright, modern steamship in the full glare of electric lights was quite a bit more startling and anticipates the aesthetics of Ramsey Campbell. George Romero could not set his zombie film *Dawn of the Dead* in a shopping mall until there *were* such things as shopping malls, nor would the story resonate until shopping malls and consumerism had made changes in American culture.

Art of any kind is part of a long dialogue with previous art. It also is a product of its time, even when it evokes images from the remote past. (You only need compare, say, Lew Wallace's *Ben Hur* with a modern historical novel set in the same period to see the difference.)

Weird Tales® is part of such a dialogue. It continues a tradition, but not as a dead limb. We're not looking for the superficially trendy, but for the solidly entertaining, for the kind of story which (to steal a phrase from, we think, Ellen Datlow) leaves the reader with "a lasting object of contemplation." The problem with being very "now" is that you soon become very "then," as exemplified by a story by Henry Kuttner, published in 1938, about the discovery of the

planet of the Jitterbugs. No one cares about that story now, but Kuttner went on to write classics, which were not only of their time but have lived well beyond their time.

Now there will be some changes under the newly restored Triumvirate of Scithers, Schweitzer, and Betancourt. For one thing, to make it even more obvious that we have always been open to new and unknown writers, we have begun putting author-blurbs at the ends of the stories. We have tended to publish one or two first-sale writers in just about every issue for the past 18 years — many, many new writers — but we hope we will encourage even more new writers if we show them that ours is not a closed market; you do not have to know the secret handshake to get in. We do read unsolicited submissions.

We'd like to know how you feel about one question: As long as we're bi-monthly, it is possible to run two-part serials. How do you feel about this? Our own feeling is that we should have perhaps one a year, between the special-author issues. There aren't a lot of markets for novellas, so we're sure we could find plenty of good ones.

We get letters and would like to get more of them. E-mail us at:

<weirdtales@comcast.net>

(with the phrase "Weird Letter" in the subject line, please.)

Chronicle is the Science fiction, Fantasy and Horror monthly news and trade magazine; no one else gives you the kind of extensive coverage that we do. In every issue we review lots of books, we bring pages and pages of news, we have a regular market report and a monthly buyers guide, and we don't stop there. We're the only place that you'll find Jeff Rovin's "SF Cinema," Mike Jones' "Short Cuts," and Alan Dean Foster's movie reviews. No one else even comes close to our in-depth feature articles that outline the state of the field. We now bring the science fiction world to you in full color. Don't be surprised by the future of genre publishing, be part of it! Get the inside information that no one else gives you, subscribe today! And it's all backed by the DNA guarantee: If you're ever unhappy with your subscription at any time, just cancel it and we'll give you a refund on all unmailed issues, no questions asked.

We're so sure you'll be happy with *Science Fiction Chronicle* that we're willing to give you the first issue for free. Once you've looked over the issue, if you're not completely happy with it just cancel your subscription and we'll give you a full refund. Since this subscription is risk-free, there's no reason not to take advantage of this special offer. We've never made a better offer, and there's never been a better time for you to subscribe to *Science Fiction Chronicle*.

❏ Yes, I want a subscription to *Science Fiction Chronicle* and send me my free issue!
❏ 1 yr. (12 issues) of *SFC* $44.95   ❏ 2 yrs. (24 issues) of *SFC* $79.95
❏ 1 yr. (12 iss.) of *SFC* (1st class) $58.00   ❏ 2 yrs. (24 iss.) of *SFC* (1st class) $106.00

Name (please print) _____

Street Address _____

City, State, ZIP _____

❏ Visa ❏ MC # _____ Exp. _____

Cardholder Signature _____

Please make your check or money order payable to DNA Publications and mail to P.O. Box 2988, Radford VA 24143-2988
Rates valid in USA only. For international rates, visit our website: www.dnapublications.com

Editorial Book Reviews:

In the Palace of Repose by Holly Phillips. Prime, 2005, hardcover, 203 pp. $29.95; trade paperback, $15.00. Prime is an imprint of Wildside Press edited by our own Sean Wallace, so maybe it is a tad nepotistic to review this here, but we break the rules now and then. This is a (mostly) brilliant book by a new writer who may well become quite important. There's just a touch of apprenticeship in this collection of nine stories, only two of which have been published before. "One of the Hungry Ones" is more confusing than "delicately horrific" as the flap copy promises, and maybe the male narrator of "By the Light of Tomorrow's Sun" isn't quite as convincing as some of the author's female characters (though the story is quite good anyway), but beyond that Phillips seldom misses a note. The title story, her first major publication, originally from *H.P. Lovecraft's Magazine of Horror* is exquisite, and, we admit we're jealous. It's the perfect *Weird Tales*® story about an ancient Mittel-Europa bureaucracy which had kept a dread (and perhaps dreadful) god imprisoned for centuries, and now faces a crisis because no one believes in the god anymore and the funds have been cut. "The Other Grace" is a wonderfully eerie story about a girl who loses her memory, and develops the idea that she is in conflict with her "other self," the former self she once was. Great stuff, very lyrical. Now writers like this have proven to be one-day wonders; but unless Ms. Phillips's brain is suddenly carried off to Yuggoth in a jar, we do not think she is going to meet such a fate. Hers is a name to watch.

The Best of Xero edited by Pat and Dick Lupoff. Tachyon, 2004, hardcover, 272 pp. $29.95. This one may take a bit of explaining to the uninitiated. Once upon a time there were fanzines, real fanzines, not what media fans call "zines," but (at their best) intelligently edited, lively journals of discussion and debate, aimed at the inner circles of the science-fiction and fantasy community, never reaching more than a few hundred at most. They had all the spontaneity of an internet discussion board, but were far more substantial, publishing full essays, not just quick comments. They were usually mimeographed, an arcane process that involved messy black ink, pulpy paper called twilltone, and wax stencils typed upon with a mechanical typewriter. While some fanzines still exist today (though few are mimeographed) they are not nearly as central as they once were. Back in the early '60s *Xero* was the place to be. Dick Lupoff was the now-successful novelist Richard Lupoff, then at the beginning of his career. He and his wife Pat put together a brilliant little magazine about anything they were interested in. They were interested in comics. A series of articles from *Xero* was later expanded into what is still one of the best books about early comics, *All In Color For a Dime*. But there was more. The essence of fanzine editing is to get a dialogue going, and in the course of the conversation readers of *Xero* heard such voices as Harlan Ellison reviewing *Psycho,* James Blish writing about his days of working on *Captain Video,* Blish again reviewing *New Maps of Hell,* Donald Westlake angrily quitting science fiction and setting off a fire-storm of response, Lin Carter as a serious scholar-critic discussing the Jules Verne revival and later as a fan parodying Fu Manchu, a long piece about Clark Ashton Smith by the otherwise unknown H.P. Norton — and we can't resist quoting the title of one Avram Davidson item: "He Swooped on His Victims and Bit Them on the Nose." Other contributors include Otto Binder (half of Eando Binder), Ed Gorman, Bob Tucker, Roger Ebert, L. Sprague de Camp, Roy Thomas, and many more. It must have been a joy to have been a part of *Xero*. Now, at least, we have this wonderful time-capsule of a book, a glimpse into a lost world.   Ω

THE DEN

by Scott Connors

Lovecraft: Tales edited by Peter Straub. Library of America, $35 (hardcover) ISBN 1-93108-272-3

H.P. Lovecraft: Against the World, Against Life by Michel Houellebecq. Believer Books, $18 (trade paperback) ISBN 1-93241-618-8

Letters from New York by H.P. Lovecraft. Night Shade Books, $40 (hardcover) ISBN 1-89238-937-1

Letters to Rheinhart Kleiner by H.P. Lovecraft. Hippocampus Press, $20 (trade paperback) ISBN 0-97487-895-2

The Lovecraft Chronicles by Peter Cannon. Mythos Books, $15 (trade paperback) ISBN 0-97285-453-3

Out of Mind: The Stories of H.P. Lovecraft. Starring Christopher Heyerdall. Directed and written by Raymond Saint-Jean. Volume 3 of the H.P. Lovecraft Collection. Lurker Films, $19.95 (DVD) ISBN 0-97451-032-7.

H.P. Lovecraft's Favorite Weird Tales, edited by Douglas A. Anderson. Cold Spring Press, $14.90 (paperback) ISBN 1-59360-056-9

The Terror and Other Stories by Arthur Machen. Chaosium, $15.95 (trade paperback) ISBN 1-56882-175-1

The Life of Arthur Machen by John Gawsworth. Friends of Arthur Machen/Tartarus Press. ISBN 1-87262-181-3.

The House of Sounds and Others by M.P. Shiel. Hippocampus Press, $20 (trade paperback) ISBN 0-97487-896-0.

It is not possible to overestimate the importance of Howard Phillips Lovecraft to the field of weird fiction. This statement may seem axiomatic to the readers of *Weird Tales®,* but nonetheless it needs to be restated every so often lest we allow fond familiarity to breed complacency. Two recent publications, a prestigious collection of his stories and an exciting critical study by an iconoclastic French intellectual, serve to dispel that complacency.

It is debatable whether or not there still exists so nebulous a concept as a "literary canon"; but to the extent that it does, Lovecraft might be said to have entered it when the Library of America included two of his "Fungi from Yuggoth" sonnets in an anthology of American poetry. This thick collection of **Lovecraft: Tales,** which falls in sequence of publication between Theodore Roosevelt's *Letters and Speeches* and Louise May Alcott's *Little Women,* would have both impressed him with its dignified appearance and classic design, and astounded him (and Edmund Wilson) by its very existence. Within its 838 pages, it presents twenty-two of his stories, selected and annotated by best-selling horror novelist Peter Straub.

Included are the short novels *The Case of Charles Dexter Ward* and *At the Mountains of Madness,* in the definitive texts established by the preeminent Lovecraftian S.T. Joshi; in fact, this collection represents the first time that "The Shadow out of Time" has appeared between hard covers since the discovery of the original manuscript in the mid-1990s, making this collection a must for even the hardcore afficionado who already owns the Arkham House editions edited by Mr. Joshi. (Mr. Joshi is to be commended for his coöperation with this project, allowing his work to be used even though he was bypassed in favor Mr. Straub, who was perhaps regarded as more marketable to the general reader).

Straub's selection is basically sound, although I question the inclusion of such a weak story as "The Lurking Fear" when such a lovely paen to old New England as "The Festival" is omitted. Also, I cannot be convinced that the inclusion of "Herbert West — Reanimator" was not an attempt to cash in on the popularity of the Stuart Gordan film based upon it. The earliest story included is "The Statement of Randolph Carter," written in 1919, while the latest is "The Haunter of the Dark," Lovecraft's last story written entirely by himself, and provides adequate representation of all phases of Lovecraft's creative life save one: Straub deliberately omitted any of his so-called "Dunsanian tales," a serious misnomer since Lovecraft was writing in that style before he discovered the tales of the great Irish fantasist Lord Dunsany. At least one of these stories, "The Silver Key," written during the great burst of creativity precipitated by Lovecraft's return to Providence after the two years of his "New York exile," is arguably one of his finest creations, and to exclude this poignant and lyrical piece is to present an incomplete impression of his life achievement. But all of the other greats are here, from the gruesome discoveries beneath Exham Priory in "The Rats in the Walls" to art appreciation à la "Pickman's Model," from the near-pastoral evocations of New England in "The Colour out of Space" and "The Whisperer in Darkness," to such nightmarish portraits of New York as "He" and "The Horror at Red Hook."

Mr. Straub also provides cursory notes on each story, along with a detailed chronology of Lovecraft's life, although like most of the Library of America volumes this one lacks an introduction, the idea being not to influence unduly the neophyte reader with the opinions of alleged authorities, but to allow the texts to stand on their own merits.

Michel Houellebecq (pronounced "Wellbeck"), author of *Platform* and *The Elementary Particles,* is a prominent French author who won the prestigious *Grand Prix national des Lettres Jeunes Talents* in 1998. *H.P. Lovecraft, contre le monde, contre la vie* was his first book, published in 1991, and it has just been published for the first time in an admirable English translation by Dorna Khazeni as ***H.P. Lovecraft: Against the World, Against Life***. The reader would do well to bear in mind that in the author's own words this is less a formal critical study than his first "novel," with Lovecraft as the protagonist. A number of myths are repeated within its 119 pages (the rest of the book consists of an admiring introduction by Stephen King and reprints of "The Call of Cthulhu" and "The Whisperer in Darkness"), illustrating the truth of John Ford's observation in *The Man Who Shot Liberty Valance* that "When the legend becomes fact, print the legend," but these do not adversely affect the thrust of his argument. When Houellebecq writes "Absolute hatred of the world in general, aggravated by an aversion to the modern world in particular [. . .] summarizes Lovecraft's attitude fairly accurately," we realize that this likewise summarizes his thesis. And to be fair, there is much to be said for this as he expounds in detail. Certainly when he writes that Lovecraft was less than enchanted with life he is on solid ground: witness the statement in Lovecraft's Commonplace Book that "Life is more horrible than death." Unlike many earlier Lovecraft scholars he not only does not downplay his subject's racism, he positively embraces it. This is perhaps a reflection of Houellebecq's own personality: he remains a controversial figure in France, having been tried (and acquitted) in 2002 on charges of inciting racial hatred for statements attacking Islam. Race is still an uncomfortable subject for many of Lovecraft's admirers, yet Houellebecq's approach strikes me as having more than a kernel of truth at its core. I do not feel that he is projecting his own views onto Lovecraft, but rather he recognizes in Lovecraft someone who was likewise able to channel this aversions into a significant artistic achievement. I take issue with his assertion that Lovecraft rejected all forms of realism, since in his latter works, the very stories Houellebecq calls the "Great Texts," rely upon what Clark Ashton Smith called a sort of "pseudo-realism," building up a sense of reality through accumulated detail in the manner of a hoax right up until the introduction of the fantastic element. I will admit that perhaps he was merely being hyperbolic, since he describes with admiration the "style of scientific reporting" adopted in these same stories. At the end he credits Lovecraft with having achieved an almost Schopenhauerian renunciation, telling us "How We Can Learn from Howard Phillips Lovecraft To Turn Our Spirit Into A Living Sacrifice," painting an almost messiah-like portrait of the Gentleman from Angell Street.

Houellebecq also remarks on how "strange shadow of [Lovecraft's] personality" continues to fascinate readers as much as his fiction. Part of this is due to his voluminous correspondence, which allows the new reader the illusion of an intimacy with the author that is highly seductive. Two new volumes of letters have recently been published, both edited by the highly capable team of S.T. Joshi and David E. Schultz.

Like W. Paul Cook, Houellebecq attributed Lovecraft's final maturation as an artist and as a person to his experiences in New York, and **Letters from New York** provides ample documentation of that experience. It is fascinating to see how his attitudes changed from his initial enchantment with the fairylike Manhattan skyline to his final Dantesque vision of "The Horror at Red Hook." Those who still consider Lovecraft to have been a recluse will be stupefied with the accounts of his active social life. Anyone who can read his account of how his room was burglarized, leaving him literally with just the clothes on his back, without sharing his sense of violation and loss, lacks empathy to an almost pathological degree. Speaking of pathology, these letters, mostly addressed to his Aunt Lillian, contain ample evidence of his racial views, and provide an excellent backstop to Houellebecq's essay. The editors also include his poignant letter to Frank Belknap Long of May 1, 1926, which recounts his emotions upon his permanent relocation to Providence. Lovecraft wrote only a few stories during his New York period, but read extensively, producing his seminal essay on Supernatural Horror in Literature. As Houellebecq observes, "Lovecraft must have felt a need to recapitulate all that had been done in the domain of horror fiction before exploding its casing and setting off on radically new paths," as evidenced by the unprece-

dented outburst of creativity he enjoyed over the next two years.

Messrs Joshi and Schultz also present us with **Letters to Rheinhart Kleiner**. Kleiner was one of HPL's closest friends from his amateur days, and a founding member of the Kalem Club, a loose-knit group of Lovecraft's friends in New York so-called because the initial members' names all began in K, L, or M. Kleiner was not an aesthete like Samuel Loveman nor an intellectual like Alfred Galpin, nor was he particularly interested in weird fiction, although he provided the model for the character St. John in "The Hound." He was an "ordinary Joe" of some taste and intelligence who played a major rôle in the socialization of the gawky misfit who dropped out of Hope High School and never emerged from his mother's home except to walk the streets of Providence at night, and these letters provide ample documentation of Lovecraft's chrysalis. The editors also provide a representative sample of Kleiner's own work, allowing us a clearer idea of who he was. They also include all of Kleiner's essays and memoirs on Lovecraft, which are by no means among the least of those we have.

Peter Cannon is both a distinguished authority on the life and works of H.P. Lovecraft, as well as one of the most distinctive contributors to the field of Lovecraftian fiction. His latest novel, **The Lovecraft Chronicles**, reminds me of the old poem "For want of a nail the shoe was lost." The nail that changes Lovecraft's life is a young teenage girl he chances to meet on a bus with whom he forges a friendship. When publisher Alfred A. Knopf solicits a manuscript for a book proposal, as happened in real life, her father uses his networking skills to put in a good word for the book, which ensures its publication to both critical and financial success. This encourages HPL to continue writing, and with a newfound financial security he is able take better care of himself so that he avoids the cancer that ended his life so prematurely. HPL travels to California when Max Sennett buys the rights to "Herbert West: Reanimator," and ends up as one of the re-animated in the film, initiating a brief career as a slapstick comedian à la Buster Keaton. He travels to England where he befriends Arthur Machen and George Orwell, and even participates briefly in the Spanish Civil War.

Although Cannon's affection for his subject is

plainly apparent, there is an undercurrent of tension as HPL's long-held beliefs are challenged, first by his young friend regarding race and class (like his wife, Sonia Greene, and his Providence protégé and collaborator Kenneth Sterling, she is Jewish) and then by his British secretary regarding his relations with women. While the overall tone of the book is light, as befits one who has raised the art of the P.G. Wodehouse pastiche to a high level indeed, there is a harrowing scene where Lovecraft's birds come home to roost. This is a work of irony, and while HPL may be the hero, he is depicted as what Northrop Frye called an alazon, "a deceiving or self-deceived character in fiction, normally an object of ridicule in comedy or satire, but often the hero of a tragedy." Lovecraft's half-joking pose as an ancient scholarly gentleman fits this perfectly. While Lovecraft's attitudes continue to evolve (he even changes his wording in "Cats and Dogs" to eliminate the implication that Blacks were not human beings), his failure to finalize his divorce from Sonia is shown to be part of a pattern of denials that finally robs him of a real chance for a normal romantic relationship.

The last portion of the novel is for me the least satisfying, for here the irony degenerates into slapstick, when Frank Belknap Long and his bride, Lyda, enter the scene. The way Cannon depicts Lyda reminds me of the Bugs Bunny cartoon about the Slobovian rabbit that Elmer Fudd's uncle sends him for safekeeping; the scary thing is that those of us who had met her can't deny that Cannon has, like Pickman, drawn a picture from life. One might well think that, given the choice, Lovecraft would have elected to die in 1937 rather than endure the highly undignified passing he suffers here. Cannon has not just written a speculative biographical novel, but has used Lovecraft, warts and all, to create a comedy of manners. If at the end it turns out to be a black comedy, nobody would be less surprised that Lovecraft himself, who wrote that "Life is indeed comic, but the joke, I fear, is upon mankind."

Lovecraft comes to life in a stunning performance by Christopher Heyerdall in a docu-drama produced for the Canadian Bravo! Arts network several years ago. *Out of Mind* opens with what appears to be Lovecraft sitting at a desk before a radio microphone, giving a lecture. He is shy and hesitant at first, but becomes more intense as he warms to his subject:

"I am essentially a static, contemplative, and objective person; almost a hermit in daily life, and always preferring to observe rather than to participate My natural — and only — genuine form of imagination is that of passive witnessing — the idea being that of a sort of floating, disembodied eye which sees all manner of marvellous phenomena without being greatly affected by them."

The film combines excerpts from Lovecraft's stories, letters, essays, and Commonplace Book with plot elements from *The Case of Charles Dexter Ward*, "The Call of Cthulhu," "Herbert West — Reanimator," and especially "The Statement of Randolph Carter" to present the truest cinematic depiction of Lovecraft's aesthetic achievement to date. Much of the impact comes from actor Christopher Heyerdall's performance. His Lovecraft is appropriately angular and lanky, projecting the air of a reserved, courteous, and, above all, dignified gentleman. *Out of Mind* continues the depiction of Lovecraft as the eccentric recluse. While this is regretable, it is understandable for both budgetary and artistic reasons: the producers couldn't afford to show all of the people whose lives were touched by the man they came to call Grandpa Theobald. They manage to suggest this impact by the device of having him as a radio personality on a newsreel, much in the manner that Algernon Blackwood actually did late in his life with the BBC. If Heyerdall's voice is not the "high-pitched piping" described by contemporaries, then like George C. Scott's portrait of General Patton, Heyerdall provides the voice that generations of Lovecraft fans always knew he had from their mental portraits of the man. Lurker Films (www.lurkerfilms.com), the folks behind the H.P. Lovecraft Film Festival in Portland, Oregon each October, have issued this gem in a widescreen presentation. Also included is John Strysik's outstanding short film *The Music of Erich Zann*, with the sound remastered for Dolby Digital 5.1, along with short features by Aaron Vanek (The Outsider and My Necronomicon). A special bonus is the trailer for the forthcoming amateur film version of *The Call of Cthulhu*, which was the hit of last year's festival. This DVD is an excellent way to explain Lovecraft to the curious, and is highly recommended.

Lovecraft listed his favorite weird tales in several letters as well as "Supernatural Horror in Literature," but up until now they have not been gathered together in one place. Now Mythopoeic

Award winner Douglas A. Anderson has collected them all together as **H.P. Lovecraft's Favorite Weird Tales**, subtitled **The Roots of Modern Horror**. This book is based upon two lists of favorite tales that Lovecraft drew up in 1929 and 1934, respectively, plus a letter to "The Eyrie" wherein he listed his favorite stories from this magazine. Anderson divides the stories up into two groups, the literary and the popular. The literary group includes Poe's "Fall of the House of Usher," Arthur Machen's "The White People," "The Novel of the White Powder," and "The Novel of the Black Seal," Algernon Blackwood's "The Willows," M.R. James's "Count Magnus," "The Suitable Surroundings," and "The Death of Halpin Frayser" by Ambrose Bierce, "The Yellow Sign" by Robert W. Chambers, "Seaton's Aunt" by Walter de la Mare, "The House of Sounds" by M.P. Shiel, and the novelette version of A. Merritt's *The Moon Pool*.

The popular group includes Paul Suter's "Beyond the Door," M.L. Humphrey's "The Floor Above," H.F. Arnold's "The Night Wire," Arthur J. Burks's "Bells of Oceana," Everil Worrell's "The Canal," and John Martin Leahy's "In Amundsen's Tent." This is an outstanding selection, testifying most eloquently to Lovecraft's generally superb taste in his chosen area of expertise. One might quibble at the division between the literary and the popular, seeing as how the Merritt novelette appeared in a pulp just as did the selections from *Weird Tales,* and one might regret the omission of any stories by Clark Ashton Smith, Henry S. Whitehead, Donald Wandrei, or Robert E. Howard, all of whose work HPL likewise held in the highest regard; but this is still one of the best anthologies ever published, and would make an excellent textbook for a college course on the genre. Anderson has provided an informative introduction as well as notes for each of the stories, exploring Lovecraft's remarks on each of them as well as their possible influence upon his own writings.

The writer whose works appear on Lovecraft's "best of" list more than even his "god of fiction," Edgar Allan Poe, is the visionary Welsh writer Arthur Machen (1863–1947). Chaosium has recently published **The Terror and Other Stories** as the latest in a series of Machen's best weird fiction, part of its line of fiction related to its popular "Call of Cthulhu" rôle-playing game. All three volumes to date have been edited by S.T. Joshi, and present an eclectic but satisfying survey of all aspects of Machen's macabre work. *The Terror* was a novel that was originally serialized in the midst of World War I, and is an early indication of how the Great War was shaping the artistic angst of a generation. It is an extremely effective account of how the natural world reacts to the insanity of that conflict, and is clearly a precursor to such works as Daphne du Maurier's *The Birds* and the Alfred Hitchcock film based upon it. Also included are a number of short stories and an essay on occultism in literature. The short stories are not up to the standards of "The White People" or "The Great God Pan" (few are!), but they are still very effective horror stories; some of them even deal with the malevolent "Little People" who appear in such classics as "The Novel of the Black Seal" and "The Shining Pyramid." Hardcore Machen readers will even find a couple of stories that originally appeared in original anthologies edited by Lady Cynthia Asquith in the 1920s and 1930s and are not included in either of the two Tartarus Press collections currently in print.

Machen's foremost champion among contemporary publishers is without doubt Tartarus Press. Its proprietor, Ray Russell, has now published for the first time a work legendary among Machen afficionados, **The Life of Arthur Machen** by John Gawsworth. Its author was barely out of his twenties when he completed this exhaustive biography of one of the most distinctive prose stylists in the English language. While Machen was alive to aid Gawsworth in his efforts, he still maintained a degree of reserve, feeling that only politicians were the subjects of books while they still drew breath. Tartarus Press has outdone itself in producing a truly gorgeous volume, which is appropriate considering that its author was himself more interested in books as objects rather than as vessels containing meaning and ideas. This is not the place to find scintillating analyses of the symbolism in "The White People," but it does contain much that is of interest. For instance, I read with keen interest about how the model for *The Three Imposters* was later hanged as a murderer!

The book itself is limited to 250 copies that were distributed to the Friends of Arthur Machen. I quote from their website: "The book is produced in association with Javier Marias, King of Redonda, and may be published in a trade edition later this year by Tartarus. At the moment this book has been published only for members of the Friends of Arthur Machen and is not available direct from Tartarus Press. Membership is available to all and for details please contact The Treasurer, Friends of Arthur Machen, 78 Greenwich South Street, Greenwich, London, SE10 8UN [UK]; For e-mail: http://www.machensoc.demon.co.uk"

I encourage all who love Machen's visions of the truth behind the veil of illusion we laughingly call "reality" to support the Friends of Arthur Machen, and I hope that Tartarus Press can bring out a trade edition.

Gawsworth is better remembered as the foremost champion of another alumnus of Lovecraft's list of the best weird stories, Matthew Phipps Shiel (1865–1947), a relic of the Yellow Nineties whose florid and ornate prose style makes Clark Ashton Smith seem like Ernest Hemingway by comparison, but whose singularly vivid imagina-

tion found great favor with both CAS and HPL. *The House of Sounds* is the latest in Hippocampus Press's series, "Lovecraft's Library," which reprints a number of rare items about which Lovecraft waxed enthusiastic in his letters and essays. The prolific Mr. Joshi is once again responsible for this gem of a collection that includes such short stories as "The House of Sounds," "The Pale Ape," and "Huguenin's Wife," all of which were praised extensively by HPL in *Supernatural Horror in Literature* and elsewhere. Also included are "Vaila," the original version of the title story from Shiel's 1896 collection Shapes in the Fire, plus the original 1901 version of what may well be the best end-of-the-world story ever written, *The Purple Cloud*. To call Shiel's prose flowery is an understatement, but he manages to create an atmosphere that is stunning in its intensity and sense of impending doom. Shiel is an acquired taste, but is well worth the effort to cultivate. Ω

MY SISTER'S HOUSE

by Parke Godwin

illustrated by Allen Koszowski

It drifted in a shadowed corner of the attic, part of the dust and smell of abandoned clothes, old paper and cardboard — and dreamed images dim and fragmentary as Itself. Now and then there came the whisper of words It could not remember, but images were clearer. Sometimes It remembered faces and raged, howled at them without a mouth to make sound. Lines of color slashed from nowhere to nowhere, but now, though there was no sense of time, It searched endlessly for something lost. Again and again, but each time the lost thing seemed about to be found, Its way was blocked. *Lost* disappeared and the dream began again in frustration, over and over until It spiraled down, exhausted, into oblivion again.

But with each coming of the weary dream, It grew stronger. Each time It remembered more and more but, because the way to *Lost* was ever barred, It screamed and hated.

"I can't go," my niece insisted for the third time. "Look, I can't get a baby sitter, okay?"

Jesus. I rolled my eyes to the ceiling as Leora's excuses splintered over the phone from Queens to Manhattan in the blunt Long Island accent time and travel had worn out of me. "So what about your sister? Polly lives just over in Little Neck, doesn't she?"

"Hey, I tried," Leora said flatly. I listened to more excuses that wore thinner with repetition. Leora's husband didn't want her to do it; good old nine-to-fiver wanted her home and dinner ready when he got there. He hated being in my sister's house anyway, and who needed a bunch of old pictures and stuff nobody had looked at for years, yada-yada. One frigging day, I thought; one afternoon and neither of them could go out to the house to pick up the last of their mother Brielle's stuff in the attic before the house was sold, but "dear" old Uncle Dave, whom Brielle had trumpeted for years as the family loser, absolutely *had* to do this much for her memory and them.

Listening to Leora guilt-tripping me —"I mean, she's your own sister, Dave. Honestly!" — I began to heat. Friends you can pick, blood you're stuck with. I'd spent so much of my life with Bree over the years. When she was sober or sentimental, I was her dear little brother; why not? I sat at her knee and took her words for gospel until I was old enough to see how she clung to hatreds like ivy to a wall. Some people are like that. You're their own darling until you start to think for yourself. In the beginning there'd been so much affection, laughter and fun between us. My big sister was my key to the glowing adult world I thirsted for —

On marriage: "Oh, it's like being let out of prison," she flourished gaily. "You can do anything you want."

Understandable: Bree grew up in the nineteen-thirties when Nice Girls Didn't, and little boys grew hair on their palms for playing with themselves.

Ten years later, the dew had apparently deserted the rose. "Where've you been, Bree?"

"Upstairs," she coughed over her cigarette, "performing my wifely duties."

Who knows when it began or if the seed was always there, but the war between us simmered, steamed and finally boiled over when I told her I was sick of her always putting down my father, sick of her clinging to old family feuds, and please go to hell. Relatively mild for our brood, but Brielle branded me a traitor to family values and didn't speak to me for ten years.

Now Brielle was a year gone, her husband Henry finally secure in his grave where he no longer cared if Internal Revenue or the banks had designs on his money, and the house was up for sale. I went to Bree's funeral, and that's the last I saw of her children except for Elaine, the only one of her daughters I could stand. What the hell, after years of Brielle's spite, venomous as it was incomprehensible to me, Polly and Leora had no use for me either, or for my father's side of the family, the Kinsellas. Brielle was my half sister from our mother's first marriage. As far back as I can remember, she hated my father, viewing Marian's marriage to Mike Kinsella as tantamount to a shameful fall from grace. Statements reaching me through Elaine reflected my sister's growing bitterness, reinforced from living in that one house forty years, leaving it less and less as years passed and her world grew smaller, becoming its voluntary prisoner until the last ride to the hospital.

Leora, still pleading over the phone. "So will you *do* it, Dave? There's no one else. I can't, Polly won't, and Elaine lives upstate."

Elaine was no fool; she got out and far away from Brielle's house and the growing spite that emanated from her mother like heat.

"Come *on*." There was a strange, life-or-death note in Leora's voice, but that was usual for her, all emotion, blurting out her feelings before she thought.

"Leora, this is ridiculous. Right now I've got troubles of my own." It was and I did, huge troubles, a freelancer's worst nightmare. In the middle of a two-book contract writer's block hit me like a case of cholera. The first long, difficult book had taken three years, finished through sheer tenacity. The second book wasn't even begun. I could barely look at the outline, kept putting off the start, hated answering letters — hell, I even avoided writing checks. The more you struggle, the worse it gets, like sinking in quicksand. You think of what came so easily before and now all of a sudden won't. You hate the sight of the computer and do anything to avoid working, but always, always beside the self-contempt there are the hard business facts of contracts signed, money paid, and time passing while you don't even dust the mouse pad.

"Uncle Dave, are you there?"

"Yeah, yeah. Leora, calm down and tell me —"

"I *am* calm, goddammit!" She paused; I heard her quickened breathing after the sudden outburst, hovering. When she spoke again, quieter, my ear caught the undeniable tension. "It's not we didn't want to do it. Polly and I went out there last week to clear out the attic."

Leora was silent so long, I nudged her. "So?"

"We can't go back there, okay?" There was flat refusal and inability in her tone. "No way. There's something about the house now, I don't know, but Polly felt it too. Dave, I swear to God. I grew up in that house. It's all I ever knew till I got married. It was okay, remember? I mean when Mama wasn't drinking or picking on us. Beautiful too with her

pictures hung over the stairs. You know how good she could paint. But last week — listen, we were up in the attic going through stuff and feeling worse'n worse, and I dropped a cookie can full of old pictures. I mean, it didn't make much noise, but Polly like jumped out of her skin and then just started crying, couldn't explain why, and all we both wanted was to get out of there."

More silence. I found myself gripping the phone too tightly. Leora was never much for cold truth, but I was hearing it now.

"I can't go back there," she finished. "Please, Uncle Dave?"

"All right already," I surrendered. Just why was frankly procrastination. Paying family dues at least I wouldn't have to face my own problems for one more day. "Mail me a key and a list of what you want from the attic."

"I already did." I heard her profound relief. "Two days ago."

That was it? I would have gone ballistic for her conning me about no baby sitter, when Leora blurted again: "Hey, it's a lot of years. You remember the number on Corbett Road?"

"Trust me. I've got social security, not Alzheimer's. And look, you little hustler —" A click on the line. Either we were cut off or Leora hung up. When I dialed back, I got her answering machine. Thanks, girl. Do me a favor and get arrested.

Crash!

At the jarring sound It stirred and woke. So long It slept like a child, dormant but living and growing in a womb of dreams that gibbered and tantalized Its sleep, dimly aware of faint vibrations. When It felt at all there was only the forever need to *find* what was lost or stolen. *Keep. Mine.* Sometimes It rose close to waking, frustrated when It reached out to grasp nothing but darkness before sinking into red sleep again.

So long It turned in restless limbo, but stronger now. The sudden crash jolted It into consciousness and rage as sight cleared. It shrank back from the two blobs of violent color swirling into motion, flowing away like stains washed out of blankness. Fading vibrations, then silence. Able to move now, surging with more power, It flowed over a jumble of shapes toward a patch of light. *Window.*

It drifted in the feeble window light with the last of barely born new strength before darkness came down again. But It would not sleep long this

time with so much anger and the *lost* to be found. *Stronger live grow move.*

Remember the way to Brielle's house? From the train station I could do it blindfolded. Up the worn steps to Bell Boulevard, down past the movie house, a world of Saturday memories. Brielle took me to my first movie there when I was little. *Tarzan, the Ape Man* with Johnny Weissmuller. Later she lived with my aunt and didn't move back to Corbett Road until she married Henry van Zant.

Time runs out differently for a child. Remember the town? It seemed then that I lived there forever. Turn down 38th Avenue, turn again on 216th Street. You could go down 217th, but when I was a kid, the Catholic gang lived there just below Sacred Heart parochial school. They picked on us Protestant kids all the time until a bunch of us rebelled one day and routed them in a pitched battle I can still remember blow for blow. I found myself taking 216th out of time worn habit down to Corbett Road along the edge of Crocheron Park. Past the house I used to live in, the Victorian with brittle old newspapers from 1913 still lining the alcove shelves, and a gas log fireplace topped by a faded Maxfield Parish print in the small, dark living room. My father's workroom upstairs that always smelled of Prince Albert or Barking Dog tobacco from his pipe. I scribbled my first "book" there, the blood-curdling adventures of a super-Dave, heavily influenced by the latest Errol Flynn movie or Saturday serial.

Down the long block of hundred-year-old homes built for ordinary families and going now for half a million, what the girls were asking and would probably get for the last stop on the block. Brielle's house.

I *so* did not want to be here. Matching my mood, low rain clouds scudded west over Little Neck Bay as I stopped by the **FOR SALE** sign on the chain-link fence that stood guard about the small, balding front yard. The front door was permanently locked for years. I went through another fence to the back door and up through the stripped kitchen to the small dining room and on to the living room. Picked clean as the rest, nude as a chewed fingernail. Polly or Leora had even taken up the carpeting. My possessive nieces would have salvaged the slate blue, cream-trimmed walls if they could; something, anything to finally call their own.

The air in an empty house is unnaturally flat,

like my own apartment when I was in England for two months researching the book I still couldn't start. It lacked the smell of me there, cigarette smoke, whisky, ashtrays, sweat from jogging before I took a shower. In the kitchen, the garlic, basil, lemon and other spices I cooked with. The breathing, blood-pumping scent of living people.

I started up the polished stairs but paused without knowing why and just sat down on the second step, letting the peculiarly empty atmosphere of Brielle's house sift in my nostrils. No, wait. Not empty, not nothing.

"Something about the house now," Leora said. Oh yes, that I could read and had for years in this place.

Long before I published my first professional work, Brielle's discontent showed itself in a narrow snobbishness verging on obsession.

My mother," she would say rather than *our* or just Mom, as if orphan Dave had been salvaged from a dumpster. "My mother Marian was descended from the Picketts and MacGregors of Virginia."

She was an equal opportunity snob. As high as she exalted Mommy dearest, she looked down from that celestial height on Mike Kinsella and his whole complacent, unbuttoned clan. "Kinsella? I looked them up." Waving her drink like a royal scepter. "Just pig-in-the-parlor, that's all. Don't deny it. I've studied that stuff for years, and why my mother ever looked twice at your father I will never know."

Aristocracy, real or fancied, didn't stop her from marrying at eighteen to Henry van Zant, a handsome young factory foreman who cared more for his daughters in his inarticulate way than Brielle ever did. That caring did not extend to me whom Henry considered a pain as a child and quite useless thereafter. I returned the affection. Among his associates, Henry was known for a life-of-the-party sense of humor that leaned heavily to bedrooms and body functions. We avoided each other politely.

Something about the house — ever been in a permanently unhappy house? Planks and beams are living wood that soak up all the anger, frustration, screaming and tears that cut themselves into the walls like a recording needle. As the years went by I came here less and less. Henry and the girls lived with Brielle's constant put-downs and discontent until none of them really talked to each other, the growing daughters starved for affection, learning to grab for it anywhere they

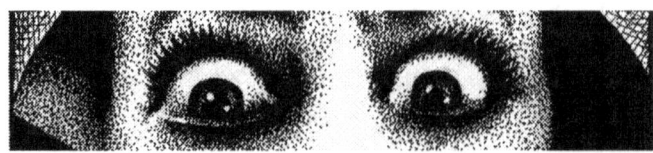

could, back-biting each other out of rivalry that congealed to dislike and distrust around the virulent hub of Brielle who never wanted any of them and said so often enough. Said it over and over until she corroded to menopause, never painted anymore, drank her breakfast, and went "strange."

Some women take change of life in stride: Okay, Life, it was a great ride but I'm just as happy to be done with the monthly curse and Tampax, or waddling around with a kid in the baby box for nine months. Others, feeling they were never fulfilled, see the crone image of middle age loom horribly and know there'll be nothing else, because Now is the whole short-changed lot, and what was once full of young promise curdles and goes sour. Goes strange.

Even dinner in Brielle's house came to be an ordeal. She'd put it out on the table, not eating much herself, just posed there with a drink, glaring at Henry or whichever daughter pissed her off most that day. For years afterward Elaine had to eat so slowly that her food was cold long before she finished, still messed up from sitting fearfully at her mother's table, expecting to be attacked for no reason.

"When I was still little, Mama started to go weird."

I saw that when I passed through about then with my first wife, Jane. (There was a second wife later and briefly, and that's all I intend to say about my married life, except that I had no talent for it). We were at dinner when Brielle scraped her chair back abruptly and rose, drink in hand. "They're here again. I know they are."

"Who?" I asked, but my sister vanished into the living room; then the creak of risers as she went upstairs. Polly and Leora exchanged there-she-goes-again looks. Brielle had only picked at her dinner as usual, preferring to drift from room to room with her ongoing monologue, leaving the last of it behind, usually for Hopeless Dave, like a bee sting stuck in my skin.

I tried again. "Henry? Who's here?"

No help there. Henry only shook his head like he'd heard too much of it already, and shoveled more meatloaf. But eight-year-old Elaine, eyes gleaming with secrets, whispered to me, "Mama says our house is haunted."

"Oh dear. What by?"

"A-leens."

Polly, the oldest, snickered. "Aliens, stupid."

After a time Brielle came downstairs, detouring through the kitchen to replenish the wine she'd already emptied twice and pausing in the doorway, drama incarnate. "They wrote on the wall. 'Get out by Wednesday.'"

Aliens serving eviction notices? No one at the table raised an eyebrow. "Who did?" I asked again, but Jane nudged my foot with her own not to make some dumb remark.

"Them," Brielle intoned cryptically, sweeping into the living room. "Them."

Of course there was nothing written on the walls, but later that day, scrawled in soft pencil, there was. YOR LAST WORNING. GET OUT.

Jane and I drove home that afternoon with a sense of relief. The illiterate alien turned out to be that little heller Elaine wanting a bit of excitement in her life, but no one could convince Brielle. She pestered their minister to come and formally purify her house with a blessing. I never discovered how a bewildered and embarrassed Lutheran pastor managed to exorcise aliens from Corbett Road, but the whole incident was pointedly dropped by Henry and the girls.

"Dave, I love you dearly, and I'm crazy about old Mike," Jane confessed on the drive home. "But Brielle does not have all her oars in the water."

"Funny you should say that."

Jane was a social worker and dealt with troubled families every day. "That is not a happy house. I mean you can *feel* it everywhere, like humidity. What it does to the girls. Henry just sort of shrugs like he gave up long ago, but those girls chattered at me nonstop, so eager for someone to take an interest in them. "My God," she concluded, staring out at the monotonous highway. "Aliens yet."

The years passed while Jane and I went different ways. Polly and Leora became distant strangers after they married. Most likely welcoming any escape, Henry died of heart failure and Brielle's acrid indifference, but Elaine stayed in contact with me, even sacking out on my couch for a week in between husbands. We talked family a lot, and she asked questions that seemed preposterous at first until I realized Brielle had completely rewritten her own life and much of family history with the Kinsellas as villains and David as the

family retard, unlikely to accomplish anything beyond head colds.

People re-invent truth when it's too painful — but one thing Elaine told me explained so much when I thought about it, one night when she was older and Brielle had a rare urge to honest girl talk.

"She told me my father could never satisfy her in bed." Not a big thing, or maybe it was. Forty-odd years can build a mother lode of frustration.

All those years growing up in Brielle's shadow. I spent nearly every Christmas with her, trusted her implicitly until I saw that somewhere along the line she'd stopped growing herself, never leaving her house, petrifying inside it until we couldn't reach each other anymore.

The afternoon light faded down; evening chill crept into the room as I sat there remembering in spite of myself. There was a young time when Brielle was full of life and fun, playing slapjack with me and clowning over the cards, or telling me stories she'd read. She had Marian's sense of drama, but that faded like the November light outside this empty house. So many things we lose along the way, like Jane, only to find others like my delayed career that mushroomed out of nowhere. With my own problems I should have refused Leora's pleas, yet here I sat in the shell of my sister's house, picking through the sad baggage of memory and feeling like a factory reject.

In this darkening room the house seemed to *sweat* gloom and defeat. *What's the matter with you? Come on, get it over with.* I drew a resigned breath and went upstairs. Past Brielle's bedroom that once housed her canopied Victorian four-poster almost too massive for the space, but Brielle demanded it of Henry along with the white satin-trimmed dressing table. On the far wall beyond the bed, the faint, pale outline in the plaster where she'd hung her portrait of Jesus, done in pastel when Brielle went Christian with a vengeance. I remembered that portrait more vividly than anything else she ever did. Not that it was very good. Brielle never traveled or mingled at all with different people, becoming complacently racist over time, partly due to Henry who never went past the seventh grade in school. They were always high-handedly scornful of "wops, spics, niggers, and kikes." Not surprising that Brielle's Jesus emerged blonde as herself with an Aryan cast of features Hitler would have loved.

"Actually, Bree, it looks like that actor Sterling

Hayden." Not too tactful. When Brielle turned on me I could see she was crushed; she really wanted me to like what she regarded as her crowning achievement.

The hurt lashed into anger: "And what would you know about art? I've studied this stuff for years!"

Art it was not, never to hang anywhere outside her bedroom. And yet in retrospect it was the best of Brielle. There was something about the portrait that clung in memory.

When I opened the narrow attic access door, it wafted me that smell all attics have of dust and forgotten things. I'd slept up there more often than I could remember, yet now something stopped me on the first step and for a moment I didn't want to climb those stairs. Then, fish or cut bait, I took them two at a time and pushed in the door on the attic feebly illuminated through the one window and the tree branches that brushed against the sill.

Stale air hit my nostrils, ten times more cloying than the living room. I yanked the window wide open, then turned to the six or seven cartons stacked in the center of the floor. Leora's list wasn't long: a framed picture of my mother Marian at twenty or so, looking far more prim and composed than she ever was in life. Polly had dibs on the good GE steam iron. I put it aside with the picture. They wanted any of Brielle's unframed works left behind, certain photographs, and forget the rest. I rooted out a pastel of Laura and Elaine as children. My search really needed a flashlight now but I paused to study the pastel in the dying light: Leora in profile, Elaine full face. If Leora had been a portrait, she'd have been a severe Holbein, but Elaine? A Rubens ready to explode off the canvas and tell you secrets just for mischief — and yet, in Brielle's rendering, both were hopelessly correct and lifeless. In none of her work was there any more than she'd dutifully learned from instructors, none of the bold, even eccentric, touches that caught a living personality. *Oh Brielle, what a terrible thing it must have been to be nearly but not quite talented at what you loved.* She worked at it less and less — "If I didn't have all these damned kids" — until enthusiasm mummified to indifference. "I used to paint for hours. Now?" A dismissive wave of her drink. "Hell, I couldn't care less."

Unconvincing; she must have cared. I heard the envy and defeat even as Brielle denied it: something loved and lost. That was the summer of '71

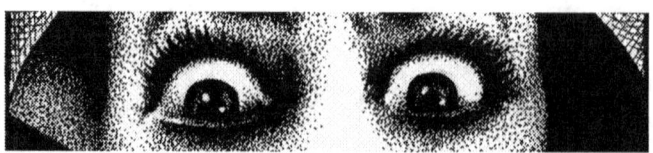

when it all tore for good between us. My first book came out, but in place of congratulations, Brielle couldn't wait to tear my modest effort apart, starting with my research into subjects "I studied for *years,* brother dear." Her standard put-down for me was always the alleged range of her "studies.". She was in her fifties then, liquor fat coarsening the long, slim body, cigarettes roughening her husky, commanding voice as she brayed her scorn at my lack of style. Stung, I countered that her taste was still mired in Tennyson's *Idylls* —

"And you haven't read anything important since Sinclair Lewis. How the hell are you qualified to judge!"

Brielle erupted from her chair, pointing imperiously to the door. "Out!" She cursed me from her house, and I muttered my way to the train station, quite prepared for more years of silence between us. What I didn't expect was the law suit or the naked truth that Brielle was now my enemy.

After my father Mike died, most of his insurance money went into Marian's chemo treatments along with most of her own. She left four thousand dollars divided equally between me and Brielle. A week after the funeral I was informed by the offices of Somebody and Somebody that the will was being contested by Brielle van Zant on the grounds of my illegitimacy, alleging Marian MacGregor had never legally married Michael Kinsella.

That gave me more than a few bad moments. Marian had certainly lived more largely and colorfully than Brielle, but this —?

Home on summer break from college, Elaine sprang to my defense, full of fire and rebellion. "I said, 'Mama, are you gonna make your own brother a bastard for a lousy two thousand bucks?' And all she did was give me that smug smile of hers and say, 'My mother never admitted it, but I know.' I mean, son of *bitch,* Dave, it's like she enjoyed screwing you like that."

I realized that in her own warped way Brielle had to, futile as it was. Marian could have left the money to me if I'd been the family dog, but Elaine's loyalty cast her into Outer Darkness with me, not that the little hellion gave a damn.

The suit was dropped after a search of Brooklyn archives confirmed my respectability. I sent a thousand of my inheritance to Elaine for school expenses and the rest to Brielle with a note subtly suggesting what she could do with it. She never spoke to me again until her last sad weeks in the hospital.

My watch said four o'clock; better hurry and finish. Should have started earlier and for sure in a better mood. Despite the cold fresh air the attic smell seemed to thicken in my nostrils. The next carton was just random papers, receipts and old grade school report cards. I pushed it aside and opened another. Well now, memory lane: my own graduation picture from junior high school, baby face and stupid grin in a blue suit and tie. Under that, the first thing I saw was on Leora's list, a framed professional 8 X 10 head shot of Brielle. She kept it on her dressing table for years. Brielle at eighteen in a plaid jacket and tam o' shanter, starting out to set the world of modeling on fire. Another studio shot in a black strapless gown, gazing down at a spray of flowers in her long, tapered fingers with the same faraway look that Vermeer always captured in his subjects. By today's standards they'd done her with too much makeup, like looking at a black and white print of an old Technicolor movie. Bree's coloring was light blonde, even her eyebrows. What real beauty she had was fleeting as spring, too delicate to bear maturity, maternity and large drinks. Her best feature was those hands, expressive even in repose. So long ago that was, before life happened to her. I blinked through a mist of memories from the girl in the picture to the last days when Brielle couldn't speak with no throat left, able only to scribble notes and search my eyes for answers with the heartbreak bafflement of a child who never could make sense of any of it, and I felt the sudden sting of tears.

I made the long trip to the hospital several times because — I don't know — despite the incomprehensible bitterness on her part and the terminal disgust on mine, there was a stubborn bond with Bree. Perhaps I never stopped needing her approval, perhaps our last phone talk when she knew she was dying — "I'm so *scared,* Dave!" — when for a moment the warring years vanished and we were close, caring blood. Love/hate dies hard. That last time I knew as soon as I saw her in the hospital room that smelled of her sickness that it wouldn't be long. She'd done her makeup carefully, knowing I'd come, but it only covered rather than enhanced her emaciated face. I'd brought some fruit Brielle would probably not eat, and a copy of my new book just published.

"Hey, Bree."

She reached for her note pad to answer. Ironic that Brielle, who could make "brother dear" sound like an obscenity, must be silent at our last meeting.

She handed me the note: *May not be able to read it. Tired all the time now.*

That was clear from the barely readable scrawl that had none of her old forcefulness. "When you feel like it," I grinned. "Great love scene on page 124. The heroine gets laid."

The ballpoint labored: *Crudely, I expect. You write like a peasant.*

"Pig-in-the-parlor like Mike."

Brielle tried to laugh; I saw that it hurt too much. *Glad you came. You're funny.*

Her smile had genuine warmth as she reached to squeeze my hand. I could barely feel the pressure of her cold fingers, but for that moment at the end of her life we were buddies again as in my childhood when we laughed together over life's absurdities, told each other stupid gross-out jokes and made inedible sugar candy that always stuck to the kitchen table.

Why don't you get married again?

"Don't talk dirty. You know I'm no good at it."

How long have you been divorced?

"Ten blissful years."

Her brows shot up in naive surprise: *What do you do for women?*

That touched me, looking at the ruin of my sister who had to ask Elaine what it was like to sleep with more than one man. "Bree girl, the saints have been generous."

We lapsed into silence then, Brielle's strengthless fingers curled about mine while the wall clock scissored off the frayed end of her life. She picked up my book with the lush painting of the nubile heroine on the jacket, and wrote: *Lousy cover.*

Lousy and unsubtle but it would sell copies. "That's my big sis. I wondered how long you could resist a put-down."

Brielle's smile soured with a hint of her old acid: *Screw you. I studied this stuff for years.*

"So you did."

As she wrote slowly, I saw the exhaustion shadow her face like sudden cloud. *You're good to come so often.*

"Hey, who else is going to keep me humble?"

I need to sleep now. Please come again? The pen

paused, hovered. Her eyes flashed something like anger at me as she started to write further but hadn't the strength. As Brielle wilted down on the pillow, I tried to read the single scrawled word. It looked like *Why?*

She was already half unconscious as I took the pad and pencil, kissed her and let my hand linger on her cheek, but there was no again. Brielle died the next day. Jesus . . .

I dropped the pictures in the to-keep bag and was opening another when I became aware of the sound, a deep throbbing felt more than heard, like a pedal tone on a vast pipe organ, so faint it might be imagination fed by my rotten mood. No, it was there, now a kind of intermittent moan like the volume on a powerful receiver turned all the way up on no signal, just the power crying through the speakers. I thought it might be wind, but the tree close to the window was dead still.

What I felt then wasn't fear but a strange physical heat that crawled on my skin and raised the hair on my neck. All right, enough. I didn't need more of this, not today. I grabbed the stuff for Leora and wiped the dust and memories from my hands. Leora could come back for anything else, but I was *out* of there, down the stairs, through the kitchen and out along the driveway to take one last look up at the white frame pile of my sister's house. I'd forgotten to close the attic window, but forget it. A burglar might get in by way of that near tree branch if he weighed less than thirty pounds, but what could he steal?

Still, something moved on that branch now. Not wind; there wasn't any, hadn't been any to make that almost-sound in the attic. Then I saw the sinuous shape of the black and white cat inching along the leafless branch. Lotsa luck, Cat. I hefted the bag under one arm — oh God, I'd forgotten the steam iron — and hurried away from Brielle's house through November twilight.

No slow drifting up to awareness now. It woke suddenly at the vibrations, terrified and then raging at the nightmare splotch of color invading the only safety It knew. It shrank back, crouching in darkness behind the clothes rack.

Sound now but still faint, registering on awareness more as vibration, but sight had grown stronger with each waking. Color — *yellow red blue* — resolved to the crude outline of a figure flowing around the vague, distorted squares in the middle of Its space. *Mine. Protect.*

The rage that made up most of Its being

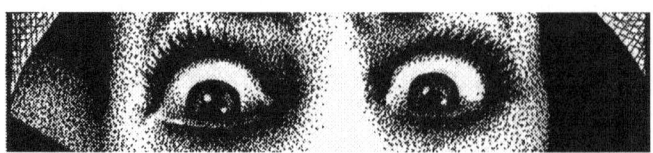

was now all. Shapeless, It launched out of the shadowed corner, reaching to grip and tear the invader, but the violent colors stretched suddenly. Instinctively It cringed away from the threat and felt strength ebb again after the one burst. The garish colors were gone now. Always before consciousness had faded after Its meager power was spent, but this time sleep did not come. It hovered in the dark corner, letting strength build again, and as it did, a word formed in Its primitive awareness —

I — and with the word came a rush of painful, rage-fueling pictures that balled Its rudimentary fists in fury. *Move. Go.*

On the tree limb outside the open window, the black and white cat peering in saw only a shadow flow across deeper darkness, raising the hackles on its neck. The cat hissed a warning.

I mailed Leora's stuff to her with terminal relief, hoping she'd forget whatever I missed and that would be that. The depression that half paralyzed me in Brielle's house lingered like a hangover while I sat day after miserable day staring at a blank page, trying to push the unborn book beyond that first line that mocked me now —

"I have no fear of what I must do."

A good narrative hook for an opening line, but I couldn't concentrate. My mind always went back, burying me in that gloomy attic and the hopelessness that came out of nowhere to drown me. I was actually glad when the phone rang. Leora; I was to be spared nothing.

"Polly says the real estate man called. Yeah, I got the package, but you forgot the iron."

"Sorry. I put it aside but forgot."

"Polly's screaming. She *needs* it."

"She can buy a new one. They're not broke." I dropped the hint like an anvil. "Which is what I'm going to be if I don't get back to work."

Leora took hints like water absorbed oil. Why should she buy a new one when the GE was good as new and no one made them like that anymore? Polly and Bobby just put all their cash in a new car and, besides, Bob was fussy about ironed clothes, even his underwear.

"Bobby's a cop. He can't write a parking ticket in wrinkled shorts? Forget it."

"Listen, okay? The realtor said the house is sold and the people are gonna close like this week, and I just know they'll throw out all the stuff we left and maybe grab the iron and whatever else they want."

"Leora, I went as a favor, lost a day of work, but that's it. If Polly needs, she can go."

A pause. When Leora spoke again there was that unmistakable overtone of fear I'd heard before. "I'm psychic, Dave. Even Polly says so. There's something — we can't go back there."

I squelched the derisive snort. Beyond being a junk food addict and avid for every astrology book in print, Leora was as psychic as a bankrupt bookie, but what she'd felt I'd known myself in that attic. "Neither can I. Tell Polly to live dangerously and buy a new iron."

"David!"

"No. Absolutely. Gotta go, 'bye."

That should have clued her, but Leora had the determination of the single-minded for whom possessions made up for love in a house where there never was any. But a few hours later, Elaine called.

"Hi, Lainey. What's happening in scenic upstate?"

Elaine's life was dramatic chaos as usual, but at least she throve on it. Her oldest daughter was being confirmed at church next month. "But hey, Leora just called me. I thought jeez, what's happened, 'cause Leora wouldn't call me long distance if her ass was on fire and I had the world's last water, but I got ten minutes of her usual crap before she got down to it. The house is being sold. Big deal, like I'll see any of the money."

"Let me guess. Polly wants the steam iron."

Elaine's surprise squeaked over the phone. "How'd you know?"

"Like Leora, I'm psychic."

"Well, I'd of blown her off, I mean, Polly doesn't speak to me even in a good mood, which is never, but then I remembered. Dave? Up in the attic on the clothes rack there's my old confirmation dress."

Oh God, not you too.

"It's right there in a plastic thingy. White with crosses embroidered around the collar." Elaine wanted it for her daughter to wear at confirmation. "Please, Dave? It's the only damned thing I want out of that house."

I should have said no, fiercely needed to refuse, but it was much harder turning down Elaine, the only living blood I could acknowledge without grudging, and her loyalty to me would probably cost her any profit from the house sale.

"Okay," I said wearily. "I'll get your dress."

"Thanks. Love you, Dave."

"Love you too." And already regretted giving in. I put down the phone and stared at the wall.

Creeping along the tree limb toward the open window, the black and white tom felt the call of adventure and curiosity. He was young, well fed, and the tag on his collar helpfully named him Whisky together with the owners' address. Banished outside for spraying on the furniture, Whisky could not resist the tree where there might be an unwary bird to snack on, and there was the open window inviting him with new challenge. He sprang lightly to the sill, then to the attic floor with a soft thump. Whisky peered about at the clothes rack and boxes. Nothing of interest, but enough to mark as his own new territory. The cat sprayed enjoyably, listening, used to the sound and smell of humans. He liked humans, but his sharp senses read nothing here —

No, not nothing, not empty. Something moved, half hidden by the tall clothes rack. A rival tom? Challenge rumbling deep in his throat, Whisky advanced stiff-legged across the bare floor, hackles rising — then froze. That presence, more sensed than seen, swirling among dim dust motes in the corner, registered unidentified threat. The cat watched, transfixed, as the outlines of a shape began to evolve out of the corner's gloom, growing and moving. Quick as the cat, the shape flashed forward between Whisky and the window, cutting off escape. Whatever was there was danger. Unhindered by human notions of grace under pressure, Whisky saw the open door and fled through it down the stairs.

It woke with a start at the faint thump of padded paws. Stronger now, stretching crude arms, flexing formlessness into something like fingers. Conscious of growing light from the window, It flowed out of the corner, then stopped as the small, darting daub of colors saw It and froze. Terror became rage. Howling, It flowed out of the corner to destroy, but the moving thing was quicker and streaked away in a blur of colors. Murderous, It pursued, pouring down the attic steps, then shrank back as louder vibrations thundered below. In this space which must be protected and the *lost* recovered, new danger was advancing. It crouched on the stairs. *Out. Get out.*

A great, frightening wall of violent colors surged through the open attic door and down the stairs toward Its own violated place that was no longer safe. Fear and shock drained energy; It let an eddy of air carry It down the narrow stairs to a new level where vague but urgent images crowded just below Its recollection, save for the primal certainty. *Mine.*

From the first waking there had been a kind of learning. Strength burned quickly, memory returned slowly. There were intruders but they must wait. Power must build before movement was possible or the lost thing retrieved. Darkness again. Rest.

Light again. Floating on a sluggish tide of air, It saw the walls while recognition drifted maddeningly just beyond reach. But . . . *this* had been here, and *that* there. It mouthed a silent scream and beat at the air in the eternal raging need that woke It in the beginning.

Sight clearer, strength growing. Turning, half visible, carved out of sunlight and dust, It saw the blank white wall sharper than ever before, and a piece of memory came into focus. Now It remembered colors here, not the shapeless nightmare of the intruding things but stroked and shaped to meaning. The sudden bright flood of memory was like a rush of living blood to Its head. The lost thing flashed clear and gleaming for an instant, and It cried out in recognition. *That* was part of *Lost* forever prayed for, forever denied. Shuddering, swirling slowly in the cold room, It wept dust-dry in the slanting sunlight and waited for strength again.

Strange: The house was cold, but as I passed up the attic stairs, a blast of enervating heat sapped all my energy and arrested me on the top step just to breathe. This house already depressed me; I passionately wanted to be done and gone. To sweeten the day, the attic reeked of cat; that black and white must have gotten in through the window. I should remember to close it.

But why did I feel suddenly so washed out?

I'd brought a suit bag for Elaine's dress, found it quickly and fitted it into the bag along with Polly's holy grail steam iron, then rummaged the cartons for anything else they might want, because no way was I going to do this again.

That junior high school graduation picture of mine: Did I really want it? I shoved my glasses

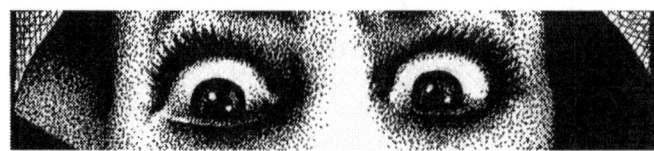

onto my nose to look at skinny boy —Dave who always needed a haircut and maybe a good belt in his smart-ass mouth. A few rows down, there was the slender blonde girl I'd had a hopeless crush on. We met thirty years later and didn't like each other much. A different world, a different time when I left the picture with my big sister whom I trusted for the answers to life, poor Brielle who never had a clue. I dropped the picture back in the box. Goodbye, kid. We wouldn't know each other now anyway.

The rest of the cartons held stuff nobody would want, mostly useless papers, receipts, Henry's old tax returns. He kept his money in the house, never trusting banks or the government, convinced they would swoop down one day to rob and ruin him. An envelope of yellowing snapshots, the girls as children, adolescent Brielle wading in Little Neck Bay —

— But at the bottom of the box, folded in half, something I'd missed before. A large square of heavy art paper, brittle with age. I opened it carefully. Yes, Leora and Polly would want this, Brielle's pastel portrait of Jesus. They would never have stripped the picture from its frame, let alone folded it so carelessly. They were awed lifelong with their mother's artistic ability, and Brielle did nothing to shatter the impression, her meager compensation for the fulfillment never reached. More likely Henry took it down in a burst of rebellion, sick of waking for years to the saccharine sight of this romanticized super-Jesus after he drove her to the hospital for the last time.

All those years ago . . . I sat there on the dusty floor with the portrait propped against a decaying carton. If there was always that crippling naïveté to my sister that rendered her conceptions inadequate and banal, there was as well the other element that stayed in my memory, an unerring sense of color that showed her command of craft rather than innate talent. Pastel is nearly as unforgiving as watercolor. Once you've made the stroke, it's there. But Brielle had learned to blend shades with a fingertip, a process of painstaking hours, so that light falling on the upturned face in its tormented exultation rendered Jesus, if uninspired, at least technically admirable. "Those who can, do. Those who can't . . ."

My God, Brielle, why didn't you teach? It would have kept you closer to what you loved, made you happier in seeing what you tried so hard for yourself burst out of a younger heart. You could have been fulfilled in that, caused far less pain and, God knows, you would have been so much more human.

Done. After a quick look for anything else they might conceivably want, I hefted the suit bag over one shoulder and carried the picture in my hand, old and brittle as it was. Descending to the living room, I heard a quizzical **mrrow** and saw the black and white cat exploring the fireplace.

"Hello, cat." The downstairs reeked of his spray, a macho feline field day. He gave me another friendly meow and came over as I parked myself on the second step. Stroking him, I remembered the open attic window, but the hell with that; no way was I going back to close it. "I had to be here. What's your excuse? Come on, I'll let you out."

As I rose, the cat hissed suddenly, a drawn out harsh sound deep in its throat. I jerked my hand away before he could scratch, but the warning was not for me. Ears laid back, spitting, he crouched, intent on something above where the stairs angled right to the second floor, emitting a different sound now that crawled on my spine as I looked up.

My glasses still on I saw nothing at first, then stripped them off. Still nothing, but the tom was flattened against the floor, rasping that sound I never want to hear again. What I saw then — what I thought I saw — could be there or not there. Pouring around the corner of the stairs came a disturbance in the air itself, a weird, rippling distortion moving down toward me. I rubbed my eyes — yes, the thing was there, coming on with that low, throbbing moan I first heard in the attic.

I couldn't think, scared numb. I backed away, not even able to run with that awful moaning in my ears that grew now to the wail of a rusty hinge in a high wind. The cat must have heard it more painfully; his spitting changed to an agonized yowl as the thing reached the last step. Against all feline common sense, the cat shot out of its crouch straight at the writhing mass, trying to get past it, remembering the only way out above.

What happened then was impossible. As the cat launched itself, the nebulous mass enveloped and caught it up. Spitting out of a strangled throat, claws flailing, the tomcat dangled in mid air from the crude shape of a hand vised about its throat. Frozen, I forgot to breathe, barely feeling my legs collapse under me as I went down against the wall. As I did, the cat dropped free, let out one final howl of terror and fled up the stairs.

Whatever the thing was, it hovered an instant, then flowed toward me. Speechless, I could only pray in that small part of my mind still working *God this is not happening yes it is happening get it away from me.*

It resolved as it closed on me, shape forming slowly out of nothing. The sound of it tortured hearing, wailing as a parody of fingers stretched down not to me but the folded picture.

Pain drove it, rage gave It strength to seize and hold the cat, resolved sight to greater clarity than ever before. The animal in Its grasp, once no more than the colors of body heat, evolved through gray to black and white. Farther away the larger shape cleared from formless colors toward definition. It squeezed strengthening fingers about the animal's neck. *Kill you. Mine.*

Something white in peripheral vision checked It. The cat was dropped as memory rushed into growing consciousness. With a fresh surge of power It flowed forward, reached. *Found.*

A long hand brushed lovingly over the white art paper, part of what had been lost. Now articulated fingers opened out the pastel portrait, knew sharply as cool snow on skin the paper's texture, remembered the image toiled over with all the love, passion and need denied elsewhere.

It started at a sudden sound from the other being close by and snarled a warning. *Get out. Go away. Mine.* But the figure didn't move, only came clearer in sight until agonized recognition crashed in on Its long torment. *You. You got what was mine.* What belonged to It by natural right. Why him? The thing, throbbing with pain, wished for the dark again where memory couldn't hurt as this One did who was nothing, had been nothing all his life, and yet the rewards went to him, and all It reaped from a lifetime of trying was pain and failure. It wanted to be at that One's throat to make him know the loss, but had always been unable. Out of death, no less a prison than her life, she screamed at him.

David!

Crouched against the wall, paralyzed beyond

fright, I heard and knew her, remembered those eyes in anger, bulging with impotent fury. Remembered hands flowed out to close about my throat. I could feel their heat as on the attic stairs, but no real pressure. As Brielle strained, the fingers weakened and she blurred again, drawing back, every moment bleeding her energy.

Close to fainting, what I could see was not all of my sister but, in the grotesque figure, all she left behind, a twisted caricature of Brielle. The long hands were hers and the distorted but recognizable remains of the fragile beauty that faded too early. What I felt then was beyond fear: awe, wonder, inexplicable guilt, but an undeniable bond with those accusing eyes. We stared at each other, live and dead, while the seconds passed like hammer strokes on an anvil as her energy throbbed in my head.

I finally managed to croak: "Brielle?"

There was something beside the hatred in her eyes: the same bafflement and unanswered question pleaded in that last illegible word she tried to finish from her hospital bed: *Why?*

"Bree," I squeaked out of a dry throat. "Can you hear me?"

Her lips moved. *Why?*

The figure drifted back a little from me. Huddled against the bare wall, I tried to make sense out of madness. I started to rise, sounding idiotic. "Uh . . . why what?"

Don't!

Not ready to argue, I wilted to the floor again below the figure wavering in and out of clarity.

Don't, she warned again.

Clear thought came hard. "I — I hear you. I know it's you."

The shriveled image of my sister couldn't stay focused, as if she were fighting just to exist moment to moment. *Why you and not me?*

I had no answer, but when she held out the picture to me, I began to understand wordlessly, where most of real human comprehension lies. The words came much later. As she fought now just to keep her hold on me, Brielle had tried all her life to be what she never could, and the emotion that flooded over my fear was a vast pity, because the questions we ask all our lives and usually die asking, lose most of their meaning in what passes for translation.

She told me more than once that our mother never liked me. Younger and more vulnerable, that might have destroyed me, but like an animal in pain, Brielle would snap at anyone or say any-

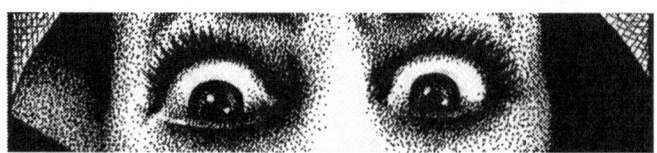

thing. "My mother never really told you how things were when you were a baby. You were her little darling." Neither was really true, but reality to Bree was what she felt at the moment, and there were my own memories from the time I was old enough to have them. Brielle ordered every day to change my diapers, walk me on my tricycle around the block, take me with her when she wanted to get out to the park with her sketch pad that Dave desecrated with baby scribblings page after page. Whenever Marian wanted time to herself, there was always convenient Brielle who had to put her budding young dreams on hold to look after the millstone of Baby David. Then she was eighteen at last, off to art school and the brief romance of modeling. Away from home at last, all the attention on her for a lovely change — then marriage and a brief time of sex without guilt before the children came, before she had a chance to know that freedom meant choices that locked her into their consequences.

I was a late bloomer, but life gave me years of a career, one book after another. Brielle's years dealt constantly with children, a dull husband and an old house that never looked good enough, too seldom relieved by an hour at the easel as time weighed her down day by day with the grinding truth that there would never be more than this, and this was pathetically far from enough. Then to see shiftless, unfocused David, whose failures she always celebrated with a drink and a sneer, explode with one book after another, stealing the prizes meant for *her*, gorging at the feast where she starved. Unforgivable. And the gnarled remains of all that frustration trembled before me now, strong enough to hate, never enough to live.

"Look," I tried cautiously, "I'm going to get up. It's all right, Bree. I won't hurt you." As if I could damage pure energy virulent enough to throttle a husky tomcat and maybe me any minute.

You hurt me all my life.

"How? For years we never spoke, hardly ever saw each other." It made no sense. I waited for that voice like a radio signal through heavy atmospherics to say more, but the remains of Brielle only glared at me, blurring in and out of definition.

That was the message, simply by being me? "That's why all your life you wrote me off as a useless joke? Couldn't be happy when I finally made it and all you could see was what you didn't get."

Almost too much to deal with. The battlefield she made of her life that never needed to be. "God, Bree, I needed you so much when I was a kid. Looked up to you, came to you for answers when Mike and Marian had none. Always when I was confused, I came to you, remember? I trusted you then. I loved you."

Even as I said it, I knew that was true and perhaps still was somewhere. "I loved you but you hated me, and I felt that growing between us year after year until I couldn't bear to be around you; until nobody could." And still that hurt to say. On the upside or down, love hurts. But her twisted features softened a little as her gaze fell on the picture.

I was always alone. This was the best of me, the last thing done before I gave up. Her form blurred again, but with a visible effort, Brielle struggled back to clarity, only to throw the agonized question at me again. *Why was I cheated like this? Why you when I was the one with so much talent?*

"Talent!" I couldn't help the bark of disillusion. How many times had I heard that from all the gifted hopefuls who were always going to but never did anything? How to give my dead and gone sister any answer the sad leftovers of her could accept? "Talent, spark, whatever, that's just the beginning. There were a hundred talents born this morning who'll always want and never be because they'll sit on their asses until they're too old to care. Because dreaming is safer than doing; there's no risk of failure. It's not the talent, Bree, it's the sweat. It's how much you'll pay to make it."

I thought of the block holding up my own work and the deeper fear that maybe I was finished, written out. Paid for the magic only to find it came with catches you never think of when it's all new. Like, no matter how good you are, there's always a new batch of kids writing now, just as sharp as you, just as driven, and hungry enough to pay what you did. I was almost sputtering now, incoherent with the hard truth that had, in its way, twisted and disfigured me as much as the remains of Brielle. "You know all talent is, real talent, the kind that makes it? It's a monkey on your back that always needs another fix, another picture, another book better than the last. And it's jealous, oh yeah. It won't allow any gods before it, locks you away with that one passion year after

year, and everything, everyone else — wives, lovers, children, all they get is what's left over."

I loved it that much.

"No, you didn't." I remembered Jane and all the fine others I sent whistling down the limbo wind while I stayed locked within the only love that ever held me. "No one ever made it without a price too high that got paid with most of their life and the misery of the poor cheated bastards good enough to love them."

The image of my sister wavered, long hands rising to cover her face. As much as she could, Brielle wept. Fear had long faded under what I felt for her now. "Whatever you told yourself, you didn't want it enough, until that day when you really believed you didn't care anymore and just poured another drink."

Lie! Her travesty of a foot stamped as in life when she was angry. *I always tried. I always cared.*

Seeing her fighting just to stay with me, I wanted to cry myself for all of it, all of us. "I'm so damned sorry, hon."

I saw her head lift as she turned about. *I hate this house.*

"But you never left it."

I don't know. It's like I couldn't. As I remembered from even her earliest letters, always something that needed fixing or redecorating, one more adjustment that might bring some satisfaction within her well-furnished prison. *I'm just here. I died here in this room.* Brielle turned back to me with a world of meaning. *One day when Henry and the girls never even noticed.*

I understood that look. A person could die that way in a moment when the future went out of them, and after that nothing really but the last hospital and the undertaker. In that kind of death, did they feel the life as it fled them? The insensitive might shrug and turn on the TV, but for Brielle, who tasted beauty once, it must have been a long dying with the monkey who let her see but never hold the only thing she ever wanted.

The picture slipped from Brielle's grasp and whispered to the floor. She was weakening seriously now; she tried to reach for it but hadn't the strength, appealing to me. *Give me my picture.*

I picked up the portrait but held on to it. "Why not give it to one of the girls? They'll want it."

We were very close now, near enough for me to see, faint under the distorting nightmare, a suggestion of her early, delicate beauty. "The new people will only throw it out."

I won't let them ever! Her nebulous hand reached to me, pleading. *Please, Dave.*

Even dead she was selfish. She'd drain the new people as she had myself, Polly and Leora. "No, damn it. Give the girls something of you to keep, something they can love."

Brielle's features became a parody of reflection before settling into the familiar vindictiveness. *Polly or Leora. They can fight over it.*

"Why not Elaine?"

She shook her head, lips twisting in a hard rictus unforgiving as her life. *I never liked her. She always fought me, the bitch.*

"Then me? Can't I have something of you at the end? Something beyond the futile jealousy and wasted life. "This is the best of you, Bree. Let me take away something more than all those years when I came back time and again even knowing there'd be an ugly fight, because there was always more than blood between us. Christ, we were never alike, but we could have been so close. We could've been family. Let me have the best of you."

Her expression altered again, as I'd seen it in the hospital that last day, washed out, unable even to hold her head up. *I can't stay much longer.*

"Please, Brielle? Let me have it."

So tired.

"Come on, Bree, fight it. Stay with me."

She did try. She fought it, her whole image writhing as she struggled and managed to drift close to me. It was her supreme effort and must have cost Brielle the little strength left. Her expression changed, softened as her arms slid about my neck. She felt dry and cold as her last energy bled away, but she made it. My sister hugged herself to me.

Give my picture a good frame.

We stayed close like that for long seconds. At first I could faintly feel her cheek against mine, then nothing. "Promise."

Will you come see me again?

"The house is sold, Bree."

Not by me! Barely audible but it rang with her iron conviction. *Come see me. I'll be here.*

I saw myself telling the new people, " Hello, I'm David Kinsella, and my sister kind of lives in your attic. May I go up?" I put out my hand to caress what was left of her. "Goodbye, Bree."

I have to sleep now.

She melted away from me, little more than a grayish disturbance in the air. The last I saw was

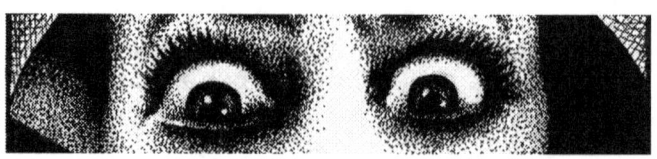

that barely discernible ripple of air wash over the lower stairs like smoke in the wind, only to sleep and wake to a house of strangers. The new people, God help them, would live with her presence until their kids became weepy and depressed for no good reason, and even the parents began to hate the place Brielle built out of her own torment. Eventually they'd sell and the house would change hands again and again until the damned thing was torn down and my sister left to herself.

I did have the picture framed very carefully under glass — so well that the art store owner puzzled over why I went to the expense since the mounting was worth much more than the picture.

"It's an heirloom," I said.

Or a gravestone, I thought, sitting in the train station that day and remembering Brielle. I tried to force my mind onto the unwritten book waiting for me, but somehow my thoughts wouldn't leave Bree who used the last of her strength to hold me close, like the family we should have been. It's true: Whatever friends you choose, you're stuck with blood. More like stuck *to*, part of and joined at the soul. All those years we fought through, hate on Brielle's side, dislike and disgust on mine, the blood lock never broke, stubborn as grass growing through cracks in cement, determined to live because it can't do anything else. As the Manhattan train pulled in, a little boy on the next bench wondered shrilly to his mother why the man looking at the ratty old picture was crying where everyone could see him.

Let them stare, Bree. I'll put a birthday rose on your grave each year, and if we do meet again on your side of the water, let's hug and have a drink and *try* not to fight. Ω

Parke Godwin (who also answers to the name "Pete") is the author of scores of novels: The Firelord, Beloved Exile, Snake-Oil Wars, Waiting for the Galatic Bus, Robin and the King, *etc. A prior ghostly novella of his, "The Fire When It Comes," won the World Fantasy Award in 1982, was nominated for a Hugo, and dramatised on TV.*

KITTY AND THE MOSH PIT OF THE DAMNED

by Carrie Vaughn

illustrated by Russell Morgan

It felt good to get away from the radio station.

At least that was what I kept telling myself as I tried to make my way to the back of Glamour, a nightclub that attracted a young and dissolute crowd. I was here for a concert. I squeezed along the wall, pausing every couple of steps as people surged back, threatening to crush me. I dodged full cups of beer and lit cigarettes. The dance floor was shuffle room only. The crowd was way past fire-code capacity.

A few hundred hot-blooded beating hearts surrounded me. It was all I could do to keep from drooling. A deeply buried part of me sensed the sweat, the heat, and thought *easy prey*. I could smell ten different brands of perfume and aftershave. Someone nearby was high on pot; I could smell it on his breath. Another had done ex in the last hour; I could smell it in her blood.

This part of me had to sprout fur and claws every full moon. Between moons, I was careful to keep my claws to myself.

I finally reached the secondary bar with the majority of my self-control intact. Red track lighting backlit a couple rows of liquor bottles, casting shadows over the usual detritus of napkins, lime slices, dirty glasses, and taps. I checked for spills on the black Formica, and finding a dry spot, hopped up to take a seat.

The bartender started to glare, but when he saw me, he leaned his elbows on the counter.

"Kitty, hiya." He was about six feet tall and a hundred thirty pounds on a heavy day. He was shaved bald, and living the nocturnal lifestyle he did, his skin was pale.

"Hey. When's Devil's Kitchen up?"

"Five minutes. Your timing is great."

"What are the chances they'll stick around after the show to talk to me?"

"When I tell them Kitty Norville wants to talk to them? They'll stick around like duct tape."

I was still getting used to the fame thing. My call-in radio talk show for the supernaturally challenged went national less than a year ago, but a lot had happened in that time. I'd revealed my werewolf identity on the air, for one. The episode put my ratings through the roof and made me one of the first lycanthrope celebrities in the country.

Fame opened doors and I had to take advantage of it when I could. I wanted to get Devil's Kitchen on my show for an interview.

The concert started late. The crowd, sensing the minutes ticking on some internal group chronometer, pressed closer to the stage. The angry edge tingeing the air intensified. Lots of black, lots of chains, and shouting.

The room went dark, all the lights cutting off at once, and the taped music went dead. Crammed bodies that had been governed by the beat of the music milled, uncertain. Then, the stage lit up. White spots glared straight down on amps and mike stands. A drum machine started up, followed by an electrified baseline, manic and terrible, like coming war.

Spirits from shadow, the band appeared. A bald guy with a ripped t-shirt and denim overalls played bass — Danny Spense. He came on stage and played like he was digging his own grave, with a kind of intense desperation, focusing only on his hands clutching the instrument, wincing in anguish.

Lead guitar, Kent Hayden, had a fascist look, slick-backed black hair, black t-shirt and jeans, fingerless leather gloves. He stared at the crowd impassively while his fingers danced on the frets of his instrument.

Together, they set up a textured rain of sound, melody struggling to escape chaos.

Eliot Ray, lead singer, leapt to the fore, grabbing the mike and pressing his mouth to the foam. He wore work boots, cut-off shorts, and a three sizes too big t-shirt with the sleeves ripped out. He shut his eyes and wailed, but it was controlled, playing with the rhythm and song; it was, after all, music. I forgot to pay attention to the lyrics.

The crowd in the pit surged toward the stage,

screaming. Fists pounded the air, a hundred bodies jumped in time with the beat.

Near me, Jax leaned on the bar, as enthralled as I was. Nobody wanted to buy drinks now.

Shouting into his ear over the music, I asked him, "How much security you guys have tonight?"

"Every bouncer on staff — and each of 'em brought a buddy. Ambulance waiting around the corner."

Over the last year, Devil's Kitchen had started headlining the club circuit. Their recent east coast tour had made news: they'd left a trail of injured concert goers in their wake. Every show they did, someone was hospitalized with injuries way beyond the usual cuts and cracked ribs of the mosh pit. It became part of the show in a way — a new kind of extreme sport, like rock climbing in Afghanistan. The more publicity they got about the casualties, the more popular their shows were. People had started following them from show to show like they were some kind of post-apocalyptic version of the Grateful Dead.

They attracted a dangerous crowd. Part of this was the music they played, heavy as granite, sharp as razors, drawn from the old European industrial scene and punk they'd cut their teeth on as kids. Most of it was the band's reputation for putting people in the hospital. Not that any of the spike-haired heroin-thin manic kids currently in the mosh pit thought that *they* were in danger of getting hurt. But they sure wouldn't mind watching someone else break a bone.

I had some theories about the band and the kind of energy they generated. They, or maybe just one of them, were vampires. Maybe not the standard blood-sucking undead, but some kind of psychic variety, feeding on danger, aggression, and bloodshed. What better venue to generate such emotions?

Eliot had more energy than any one person had a right to, leaping from one end of the stage to the other, bent over with the mike stand clutched in both hands one minute, stretched to his full height the next. He was fun to watch. I was screaming just as loud as anyone at the end of each song.

A couple of kids had started crowd surfing in the mosh pit, people passing them overhead from one end to the other. Then, one would get swallowed, disappearing in the crowd and another would spring up to take his place, riding on the upstretched arms of his friends.

They must have been four songs into the set when the first fight broke out. I didn't notice exactly when it happened; the surge and lurch in the crowd seemed like part of the natural flow. Then, a body slammed against a railing. The guy bent, his arms limp and flailing, and slid down to the floor. Four or five other guys suddenly locked together, grappling, and a space of a foot or two cleared around them. In the press of people trying to get away, more punches and body-slams crashed. Eliot kept screaming into the mike, and a swarm of bouncers descended on the crowd.

A half-dozen people, men and women, with bloody cuts streaming over their faces were dragged past me. The music faded, reverb whining over the speakers and echoing in my ears.

"We're taking a break," Eliot said as Kent and Danny were unplugging their instruments. "Round two, ten minutes. Don't move." They disappeared behind the stage.

All that blood. My shoulders tensed, hackles rising. I had to get out of there.

I jumped off the bar and ran. I climbed to the catwalk circling the pit, dodging the press of onlookers. The pit was a war zone, half the mob still thrashing to the taped music now playing, the other half trying to pick fights, struggling against bouncers and friends who held them back. At the other end of the walkway, I slipped over the rail and hopped to the back of the stage.

"Jesus fuckin' Christ, it's not even ten minutes into the show and they're already killing each other! That's a record even for us. I can't do this anymore."

"Come on, it's what they're paying for. You don't think they're actually coming for the music, do you?"

The green room was a piece of the club's storage area that had been curtained off and decorated with a minifridge and sofa. I stood at the edge of the curtain's opening and listened.

"Shit like this is not supposed to happen every show!" The angry voice — I could tell he was stalking back and forth across the space by the stomp of his boots — belonged to Eliot.

"So what're you going to do?" said the other one. "Quit in the middle of a gig? What kind of riot do you think that'll start?"

Eliot threw something and kept pacing.

"Just chill, Eliot. You're not going to quit, so stop bitching." I was guessing that was Kent. Calm and pragmatic. The third, Danny, hadn't spoken. "We're going to go back and play. The crowd'll fight like they always do. Then we'll go home. We're not paid to worry about what those jerks do to each other. Not our problem."

"Just once," Eliot said between deep, careful breaths, "I'd like to get through an entire gig without stopping because of a fight."

He threw back the curtain on his way out and ran smack into me. It was my fault; the possibilities presented by this conversation — dissention within the band, the fact that they, or at least not all of them, knew what was going on — so intrigued me that I missed him stomping toward me. We stared at each other, startled. His jaw clenched, and he looked like he was about to yell a string of obscenities.

I forestalled this by smiling. "Hi. You must be Eliot Ray. I'm Kitty Norville." I stuck out my hand for him to shake.

He looked at my hand, looked at me, his snarl twitching. "Kitty Norville? The fuckin' talk show chick?"

"Yeah."

The snarl melted into a smile, and he shook my hand. "Cool. I'm a big fan."

"Thanks." I looked over his shoulder. Kent stood with his arms crossed. Danny sat on the couch, shoulders hunched. "I'm real interested in talking to you guys. Maybe after the show? Would that be possible?"

"You want to talk to us?" Eliot threw a grin at the others. "Now we really are famous, if Kitty Norville wants to talk to us. You're, like, the Barbara Walters of freaky shit."

Kent, frowning, shoved past Eliot and me. "You'll have to set it up with our manager." He stalked toward the stage door.

"Sorry about that. I think he's got a thing against werewolves."

"Werewolves or nosy people? So — this kind of thing happens every show?" I nodded toward the chaos still rumbling from the main part of the club.

His expression tightened; he looked like he was going to yell again. But he just ducked his gaze and scuffed his boot on the concrete floor. "Yeah."

"You ever think it might be caused by something — oh, external? Like someone's manipulating things to cause the violence."

"You mean — not our fault?"

I shrugged noncommittally. "Not specifically. It's just something to think about."

Danny was staring at me from the sofa. I couldn't read anything in his expression. Just a hard, interested stare. It made me twitch.

by Carrie Vaughn

"Come back after the show," Eliot said. "We'll talk."

"No calling the manager?"

"Our manager doesn't know dick."

"Thanks."

The show must go on. The bouncers had cleared away the injured and the survivors were hungry for more. It was a wall of emotion, of anger and hate. More fights were just waiting to break out. All my instincts said to get the hell out of there — I couldn't hold my own in a fight, not with this many people. Even if I sprouted claws and fought like a wolf. I returned to the safety of Jax's bar.

Jax was nervous too, standing tense and clutching the edge of the bar, white-knuckled.

"This is really weird," I murmured.

"This is totally fucked up," Jax said, without a trace of sarcasm.

So, Eliot didn't know anything. Moreover, he was upset about the violence. There was more to him there than his image suggested. Kent seemed perpetually anxious. Who wouldn't be, with kids beating each other up over his music? And Danny — who knew what was going on in his head?

The lights went dark. The smoke came up, and the band was back, pounding its way through another set. The crowd slammed to the music as if there hadn't been a break. It was like they were on a switch, still one moment, and in the next ramming each other and screaming. Like throwing a bloody carcass in the middle of a pack of wolves. Except a pack of wolves is more organized and has manners.

About fifteen minutes into the set, with the volume and mayhem of the crowd increasing the whole time, Eliot stopped singing. The musicians carried on a few more bars, unaware that his voice was missing from the feedback. Then, Eliot jumped off the stage.

It wasn't unusual for punk and metal musicians to dive into the mosh pit. But when the others finally stopped playing, I knew something was wrong. Eliot was beating people, grabbing them and shoving them out of the way, hitting them to get their attention and forcing them back.

He was clearing a space in the middle of the floor. A body lay there, twisted and bloody.

When people saw this, they moved voluntarily. This left a circle of empty floor, the body in the middle, and Eliot crouched beside it, touching its neck, feeling for a pulse.

Somehow, there was silence when he straight-ened, scanning the crowd with a hooded gaze, his mouth twisted in a snarl.

"You people are fucking maniacs! He's *dead*. Do your puny little brains even understand what that *means?*" He looked like he might scream, his fists clenched and his whole body tensed. But he just shook his head, like he was shaking free of an insect. "I'm done," he said. "I'm outta here."

He stalked off toward the hall that led to the front of the club.

"Eliot!" Kent lurched to the edge of the stage. "You can't go. We have to keep playing."

Eliot turned, and this time he did shout. "Why? Look at that — " He pointed at the dead boy on the floor. "What are we doing that can justify that?"

Kent said, "The — the music. You know, we have to stay true."

"This isn't about the fucking music!" Eliot brought his fists to his temples, like he was going to start pulling his hair. Danny looked on, his bass hanging limp in one hand.

Kent said, "Just calm down —"

Eliot marched to the stage, reaching it in a few large strides. He grabbed Kent's guitar and, swinging it by the arm, smashed it against the floor, over and over. Still plugged into the amp, the thing squealed like a living thing, doubling over in hissing feedback. I curled up and covered my ears. Most of the clubbers did the same. Jax didn't flinch.

Kent screamed, covering his ears and staring at the broken instrument as if it had been his child. "God, Eliot — do you know what you've done?"

Eliot stood there, splintered guitar in his hand. His feet were apart, his shoulders hunched, and he was breathing hard, a grimace on his face challenging Kent to fight him.

Then, Eliot straightened. He dropped the instrument and brushed his hands. "I quit."

He started his exit one more time, but someone blocked his way.

The floor had cleared of moshing kids by this time. I'd assumed most of them had fled the club, not wanting to be questioned about the death. But none of them had left. Two hundred kids huddled around the edges of the floor, clinging to the railings, staring at the unfolding drama with hungry eyes. Pasty-faced goth chicks leaned forward; leather-clad metal heads bounced in place, like a single guitar chord would get them started again. Paramedics were stalled at the front hallway, unable to push through the crowd.

A tall, lithe man with silver hair and sharp features stood in front of Eliot, barring his way. I thought I would have noticed someone pushing his way through the crowd. Surely I would have noticed him if he'd already been here. He was taller than anyone else in the room. Or maybe he just seemed taller.

I crouched on the bar, legs tucked under me, balanced on my hands, ready to run.

Jax cracked his knuckles and frowned at the stranger.

"Who is he, Jax?"

"Bad news."

"Vampire?" Vampires didn't come to Glamour — too many groupies. And I thought I knew most of the vampires in town.

"Does he smell like a vampire?"

I straightened a little, lifting my face to the air. I could smell the fresh blood pooling on the floor. My nostrils flared. Vampires smelled dead, preserved, cold-blooded. In a crowd of pounding hearts, I could spot a vampire across the room with my eyes closed. This guy didn't smell like a vampire. I closed my eyes and took a deep breath, mentally filtering out the blood, sweat, and anger of the crowd.

"He smells . . . different," I said, confused. I couldn't put a name to any of the things I smelled in the current the stranger left in the air. "Midsummer. Starlight. He smells like —" I opened my eyes and looked at Jax. My nose tingled, taking in more scents. "He smells like you."

Jax glared at me.

Jax had been part of the local club scene for as long as I'd known the local club scene existed. He told stories about him and his droogs picking fights with skinheads back when he had a blue mohawk, when moshing was slamming, before punk had splintered into goth and industrial and rave, and before alternative was mainstream.

He wasn't a vampire, wasn't a were-creature. It had never occurred to me to wonder if he was anything other than the bartender punk veteran he appeared to be.

The drama unfolded.

"Who are you?" Eliot said.

"You've no right to question me. Step aside," he said in a rich, arrogant voice.

Wrong thing to say to Eliot. He bristled, shoulders bunching and tensing for a fight. Unconcerned, the stranger tilted his head, raised an inquisitive brow —

And backhanded Eliot clear across the floor. He landed hard and slumped like a sack of wheat.

Claws scratched at the inside of my hands. I was scared, and the Wolf wanted out.

The stranger knelt by the dead mosher, dipped his finger in the kid's blood, and tasted it. Then he stood, faced Kent, and spoke with chilling calm.

"Kent Hayden. You were doing so well. And now — silence?"

"Temporary," the guitarist said desperately. "Eliot's temperamental. I'll get him back, we'll start again. We have another gig tomorrow —"

"You said the band was with you. You said you spoke for all when we made our bargain."

"Kent? What bargain?" Danny ventured, his voice cracking.

The stranger only spared him a glance, saving most of the power of his stare for Kent, who was wilting under the pressure. "You know the one. Everyone knows it: the Devil's bargain at the crossroads."

The deal with the Devil . . . you'd sell your soul to play great music . . . music to die for.

"That explains it," I murmured. "All the weirdness — Kent Hayden sold his soul to the Devil —" And got more than he bargained for, evidently. This guy was after more than souls. He wanted blood.

Jax said, "Technically, he's not a devil. He just acts like one."

"So what are you?"

He shrugged. "Same coin, different side. Kitty — distract him. I need to sneak in the back and get the nail gun."

"Nail gun — what?"

"Cold iron. Just make a distraction."

Cold iron — as opposed to hot iron? "How?"

"Keep him talking. You're good at that." He pushed through the crowd toward the back door.

Jax was already half way around the crowd. He didn't want the stranger to see him. So . . . I had to do something. But if that guy tried backhanding me like he had Eliot, I was going to Change. When it came to self-defense, I couldn't hold it back.

Off we go, then. I reached into my pocket and turned on my mini tape recorder. Just in case.

I slipped through the crowd, ducking low and shoving until I reached the rail around the dance floor. On the other side of the rail another layer of people blocked my way. I stood on the rail and screamed.

"Eliot!" I jumped, and everyone got out of my way. I hit the floor running. What was the good of being a werewolf with superhuman strength and agility if you couldn't show off every now and then?

I skidded to a stop next to the singer. Eliot was starting to recover, pulling himself upright by gripping the rail. He held a hand on his forehead and winced.

"You okay?" I said.

"I think so."

"What are you?" the stranger said, sounding like twilight: clear voice, hinting at darkness. He was looking at me, his arms crossed.

"Radio talk show host. Can I get an interview?"

"What are you *really?*"

The air around him shimmered a little, like he was shivering with repressed emotion, a taste of coming action. I was afraid. I wanted to growl, to make him back off. But I didn't think a warning like that would have any effect on him. My skin flushed, my heart raced. *Keep it together.*

His lips thinned into a smile. He knew very well what I was.

Something touched my shoulder and I flinched. Eliot drew back his hand, startled.

"Are *you* okay?"

I was crouched on the floor, balancing on one hand, ready to spring. All I had to do was sprout fur and I was gone. I lowered my head and took a breath.

I looked at Kent, standing at the edge of the stage like he might jump off and try to run for it.

"What was the deal, Kent? What exactly did you agree to?" I said.

Kent stammered. He couldn't look at the gleaming man before him. "F-fame," he said. "I wanted fame."

Eliot laughed, a thin, almost hysterical noise. "Shit, Kent — you made the wrong bargain! You were supposed to sell your soul to become a great musician. But you sold it for fame? You, of all people. You were supposed to be for real."

"I was tired," Kent said. "I worked, I practiced — and I still wasn't good enough. What happens then? What was I supposed to do?"

"Take the easy route, of course," the stranger said.

"You have a contract signed in blood?" I said. I tried to remember every story I knew about devil's bargains, Faustian deals, the whole nine yards. There was always a loophole, right? Always a way to get out of it.

I always liked the version of Faust where he gets dragged screaming into hell.

"Of course," the stranger said, drawing a tied roll of paper from inside his waistcoat.

"I didn't sign that contract," Eliot said.

"Me neither," Danny said, raising a hand.

"Kent — did you sign in blood?" I said.

"Yes."

"You see? He, at least, belongs to me now." The smarmy bastard grinned.

For all my experience, for all that I liked to think I knew, I didn't know what to do with a soul-stealing demon. If that was really what this guy was.

"We'll keep playing!" Kent went to a second guitar case sitting at the back of the stage. In moments he was plugging the instrument into the amp. "We don't need Eliot. Come on, Danny. We can keep going!"

Danny dropped his bass.

I moved closer to the stage, so I was standing between Kent and the stranger. "Let me see if I understand this: you promised him fame, in exchange for his soul, " I pointed to the stranger, then to the guitarist. "They'd have fame, just as long as the band kept performing, no matter what." The body still lay in front of us. The kid, male, with a short mohawk and a nose ring, looked about eighteen. "But if the band stops, you —" I pointed back at the stranger. "— get their souls." No arguments so far. "So what you really want isn't their souls. You wanted the violence. The bloodshed. You get that, they get fame."

He inclined his head, smiling a crooked, amused smile.

"The music is a catalyst. The music covers up the real source. The violence comes from you. What are you?"

"An agent of chaos." He raised his left hand and snapped his fingers.

In the far corner of the dance floor, the restless energy that had been pressing against the crowd burst. Someone fell, or tripped, or shoved himself against a wall of bristling moshers. They reacted instantly by beating on the assailant. His friends came to the rescue, and a full-blown fight erupted. Half a dozen bouncers waded in and were overwhelmed. The shouts of the crowd were deafening.

"Stop it!" Behind me, Eliot screamed with berserker fury. "Make it stop!"

Fists curled into hammers, he rushed the guy.

In a real fight with a normal human, Eliot would have pounded into the guy, pummeling his head, overpowering him with sheer brutal fervor. But the stranger wasn't human. He merely held out his hand and swept Eliot aside. Eliot went tumbling back the way he'd come. He lay still.

The stranger looked at me, and I held my place. The fights were still going on around us, the crowd moshing without music, keeping its own violent rhythm, slaves to this being's power. I was hemmed in.

"I can make you fight," he said, his voice low and taunting. "I can make you Change, turn on the crowd, and rip out the throats of everyone here."

I believed him and knew I'd do better to let him smack me unconscious. So I did.

At least, I tried. I rushed him, much like Eliot had. I didn't know what I was hoping for. Jax said to distract him, so I did. I thought, if he knocked me out at least he couldn't make good his threat. Maybe he was bluffing, but I couldn't take a chance on him making me hurt people.

I forgot one thing: I was a lot tougher than Eliot. As a lycanthrope, I could take more abuse, I healed faster. The blow that had knocked him unconscious, knocked me to the floor and pissed me off. Rather, it pissed off my Wolf. She'd been itching for a chance to run loose all night. So now, in the name of self-defense, she took it.

The claws sprouted, and I lost it.

. . . the fur is free, the claws are free. Blood on the air smells sharp. But sharper is the figure of a creature. He glows, shining and dangerous. Hackles rise and finally she can growl, loud and fierce. She braces, backed against the wall. Time to fight. Find his throat. Muscles tense, and like a spring she's away, launched from a standstill, flying at him. Teeth bared, claws ready to rip.

And he flings her away. His fist catches her under her ribs and she yelps. She sprawls on the floor, splay-legged and ungraceful. He's so much stronger, no way can she win.

But she scrambles to her feet and tries again.

Someone shouts. Familiar voice. Her ears prick and she turns, just as the enemy kicks her hard with a boot like steel. Hits the wall, vision flashing. Shakes her head and looks for the next blow.

Another figure is there. Shimmering and strong. Raises a hand — he's holding something. And the thing flashes with power, over and over. And the enemy falls, screaming.

She huddles, hackles as stiff as they can go, not sure which of them to hate.

by Carrie Vaughn

The newcomer looks at her. She growls. If she could run away she would but she can't, so she'll fight.

— Kitty, it's me. It's Jax.

The familiar voice. In another life she knows that voice. But he smells like the enemy.

— Kitty, come back now. Change back.

In spite of herself, she listens. She blacks out.

I woke up not knowing how much time had passed. Time moved strangely for the Wolf. What was it they said, seven canine years for every human one? I was comfortable, and that was good. Warm, head resting on a friendly lap.

And that, so incongruous with my last memory, was disconcerting. I sat up and found myself wrapped in a heavy leather trenchcoat. Eliot was there, holding an ice pack to his head with one hand. His other hand rested on my shoulder. It was his lap I'd been using as a pillow.

"You okay?" he asked.

I didn't really want to know how I ended up like this. I settled back, snuggling more firmly into the trenchcoat. I was, of course, completely naked under it.

I smiled at Eliot. "I think you just passed the lycanthrope equivalent of the drunk test."

"Huh?"

"The drunk test: if you get throwing-up drunk in front of a guy, and he's still there when you wake up, he's a keeper." I shrugged, indicating my post-lupine state. "If you turn into a wolf in front of him, and he's still there when you wake up . . ."

His blank expression took on a more thoughtful quality, lips pursed and brows raised. "Hm. How about that?"

I looked around. The club had been cleared. Somehow, they'd gotten everyone out. The kid's body was gone. The stranger was lying spread eagle on the floor. I inched closer to get a better look.

He'd been nailed to the floor — long iron nails driven through his hands and ankles. Another dozen nails protruded from his chest. He was gasping for breath, but not dead. The wounds smoked, but they didn't bleed.

Jax stood over him, holding a nail gun. He was talking to him, the words angry and spitting. It was a language I'd never heard before. Then Jax grabbed his collar and pulled him to his feet. The nails popped out of the floor. The stranger yelped and cowered where Jax put him.

Next, Jax went to the stage. Danny was pressed against the wall of amps. Kent still stood at the edge of the stage, trembling. He'd dropped the guitar. Jax took his collar and hauled him off stage.

In English he said, "I'm sending him back Underhill. You're going with him. He was right — you signed the contract. You belong to him."

"But — but — but —" Kent didn't get out more than that. Jax shoved him at the stranger, who gathered him in an embrace. Kent started screaming.

"Tithe to Hell, man," Jax said.

The stranger disappeared, taking Kent with him.

The room was very quiet after that.

I stared at Jax. I filed through my mental catalogue of folklore. When I became what I am, I had to reevaluate what I'd previously considered to be fable. Fairy tale. I had to wonder where the truth of them lay.

"What are you?" I said, more than a little awestruck.

He gave me a wry look — not unlike the stranger's crooked grin — with narrow, knowing eyes. When he answered, it was in that odd language, complex and musical.

I sighed. I should have known better than to expect a straight answer. At least I could guess now why vampires didn't show up here. Someone tougher was guarding the place. Glamour.

My clothes were in a pile nearby. I reached for my jeans and the tape recorder in the pocket. Still going. I stopped, rewound, and played.

Nothing. Static. Not even the screaming of possessed moshers. Damn.

So there was only one thing left to ask. "Any chance you'd do an interview on my show?"

Jax smirked. "Not a chance in hell, Kitty." Ω

Carrie Vaughn's entertaining first novel, Kitty and the Midnight Hour, *has just been published by Warner Aspect. Two of the chapters first ran in* Weird Tales.

Her fiction has also appeared in Realms of Fantasy, Talesbones, All-Star Zepplin Adventure Stories, *and elsewhere.*

LOST

I found a skeleton
one afternoon
in an old coal bin
in a barn that is seldom used
low in the dripping recesses
of the evernight cellar

His bones made frames
for spider webs
a delicate portrait
of forgotten memorey
morbid weavings in silk
the only garment
he has worn in years

— George Filip

HALLOWEEN KILLER SONNET

In jowly, chalk-white mask with unkempt hair,
    And dark blue overalls, he plods along,
Through endless 'burbs, homogenized and square
    Like him — a faceless demon out of Jung.
This small-town Midwest horror and his knife,
With which he sheds the blood of horny youth,
    Sheds with it all the gravities of life,
Of sagging flesh, and slow-decaying tooth.
    And thus his victims never have to know
The death that sets in long before you're dead;
    Affixing them in timeless afterglow,
    He won't grow up; he will not go to bed.
Is not our Heartland's heartless Boogeyman
    No less a post-pubescent Peter Pan?

—M.V. Moorehead

SEVEN HOURS FROM TERMINI

by William Alexander

illustrated by Russell Morgan

I don't know why I told her who I am. Might have been the wine, but I think my lapse of discretion had more to do with being on a train. Trains are liminal, in the betwixt and between, and while on board you're in transition from one solid, real place to another. In the meantime you're nowhere in particular.

This particular nowhere started out as a station in southern France and would eventually become Rome sometime tomorrow morning. The night outside was dark, no moon through our single window. Light in the compartment had flickered and died an hour ago, at which point she'd lit two prayer candles stolen from a cathedral and offered to open a bottle of wine stashed in her pack. She was clearly enjoying the flirtation while in the safe company of a sleeping nun in the cabin's corner. We spoke English. A red maple leaf patched onto her one threadbare bit of luggage marked her as an acceptable tourist to European society, neither German, American nor Japanese.

"You're Apollo?"

Not incredulous, merely clarifying. I should have kept to my magazine, but she was of smooth voice, clever wit and the sort of skin that particularly enjoys being seen with candles.

"Apollo, as in Greek god of music and manliness and mice?"

"And of health and of prophesy. Yes." I paused with a paper cup of Merlot halfway to lips. "Mice?"

"Priests of Troad kept mice under the altar in Apollo's temple." She sipped her wine and asked, without visible sign of scorn, "Don't you remember?"

A classics buff. Had she betrayed any hint that she was making fun of me, I might have lost my temper and done something suitably wrathful and godlike. Time was when I might have. "No." Sip. "No, I don't remember mice."

I might have told her because I'd figured that belief, or the lack of it, wouldn't bother either of us. An hour or so earlier our conversation had begun in the usual ways, with questions of Where From and Where To and bits and pieces of the places in between. One usually speaks of places while being nowhere in particular.

"Have you seen Carcassone?" she had asked. Her name was Ann, I think.

"No. I've heard that inside there's nothing but plastic swords sold on every cobblestone corner, not to mention the only bad food to be had in all of France."

"Mmm," she mumbled assent around a mouthful of Merlot while digging in her pack. "You shouldn't actually go inside the castle. It's better to wander through the ordinary town that keeps it under siege, looking for it while pretending not to. If you use a compass rather than a map then you know which direction to go in but are never entirely sure about the way, and eventually you'll round a corner and find it."

She pulled out a sketchbook, which she opened to the last page marked before handing it to me. The book held a pencil sketch of stone walls and towers on a hilltop, fortified to keep chivalry safe from the cynical.

"You just stood there, drew the castle and left again?"

"Yep." She grinned as she took back the book.

"Nice sketch. Do you have an aversion to cameras? Don't want to steal the soul of a place, or just trying to avoid looking like a tourist?"

"Neither. Someone stole my camera back in Paris."

"Oh."

She spoke up after a minute or so of mutual contemplation of the window, saving the conversation from otherwise certain, silent death.

"When I was little," she began, "I grew up in the sort of suburbs which have enough trees to almost hide the fact that they're suburbs. I used to hunt for places where you couldn't quite tell the end of one backyard from the beginning of another, and trees would hide the next set of houses. I was sure that if I could cross those boundaries at just the right place and time, I'd make it through to Somewhere Else rather than into the next backyard. Maybe the sort of somewhere else that had castles in it."

She shrugged, put away her book and looked back to the window, though there wasn't much to see except for varying shades of dark. She wondered, later, if Jove would welcome us to Rome with good weather. I couldn't help saying that Zeus was dead long before the Romans called him Jove.

"How did he die?" she asked. Interested, or at least amused. "That's a myth I've never heard."

"No," I said, "this one never made it into myths." *And why start now?* whispered a little voice of my own, but the rest of me was distracted by a single lock of her hair. She kept tucking it up behind an ear, from where it would gradually work itself free again with every slight movement of her head. As I watched it fall forward and across her face for the third time since I had first noticed, my memory set to work. I began by trying to think the story into rhyme and meter, but in English such bardic practices always work better on paper than they do aloud. It occurred to me that I was drunk.

"Athene's son killed him." Now there was a beginning. Should've at least said, 'once upon a time,' because then you're allowed to talk about gods and dragons and the like. Gives you permission.

"Athene was a virgin."

"Was. She never told me about how that ceased to be the case. I doubt she told anyone. Other gods tended to be afraid of her and she never took to our father's taste for frolicking among mortals, so I haven't a clue who, or what, she might have found worth bedding. Hephaestus tried to take credit, but nobody believed him."

The nun stirred briefly and muttered something unintelligible, Ann reached into her pack and pulled out a thick, Irish-looking sweater to hold off the pre-dawn chill, and I reached for some ragged bits of memory to tie together.

"I remember running into her in a marketplace at Delphi, both of us mortal for the day. I was pretending to be a child in order to hear a street poet, while Athene was walking in the shape and semblance of an old woman. She ambled my way, and spent a minute or so in absentminded small talk before asking if I knew an elderly couple, preferably of the reclusive, sheep-herding sort, who might be familiar with the oldest laws of hospital-ity. I told her of a certain house in the eastern hills where such folk could be found.

"Now, the wife in this particular couple knew the old ways, among them rules that warn against turning from one's hearth any woman about to bear child. A mother's curse had been known to cause illness, horrible weather, plagues of small woodland creatures and so on. So when a mysterious woman arrived in the night and asked leave to give birth in their home, the red carpet was unfurled."

"Is that an *Agamemnon* reference?"

"Definitely not, now stop showing off. Anyway, after the godling was born Athene mentioned to her hosts that she couldn't help but notice the lack of strong young offspring to care for them in their declining years. They took the hint, and the child, and pretended not to notice the woman turn into an owl some distance from the farmhouse."

"Did she tell you about it afterwards?"

"No. I was the fire in the hearth, and saw it all." I made the candle flames flutter in a draft, just for cheap effect. "She probably knew I was there, but we never spoke of it. I didn't see the kid again until he came to find me."

"How'd he manage that? I would have thought that gods were more difficult to find."

"You managed, didn't you?"

"I wasn't looking for you."

"Well, neither was he." My throat was dry. I poured another cupful. "The lad was seeking his fortune, asking divine advice after his foster parents had died and he'd failed to turn shepherd. Fate might have forgotten about him if he hadn't put himself back into it by having his fortune told, and back then it was my business to know whenever the future fixed itself inside a proclamation."

"Was? So you're not in the prophesy shtick anymore?"

"No."

"Not even minor fortune telling? Scrying in tea leaves on the side?"

"No."

"Care to read my palm, maybe?"

"No."

Lights from some town or other floated past the window. I turned to look, a human reflex, a habit of seeming mortal. In biology, most things that move are either edible or might think you are. When I looked back, she was offering a bit of bread. "No thanks. Gods don't eat much." French cuisine had been difficult to avoid, but stale crust I could do without. Once begun, mortality can be a hard habit to break.

"Oh," she said. "Would it help if I sacrificed it?" She held the bread over one of the candles.

"Probably not. The smell of burnt toast isn't nearly so pleasing as a roasted offering of oxen."

"Can't help you there." She bit off a chunk. "So you told him who he was?" At least, that's what I think she said.

"Told who?"

"Whasizname. Athene's kid."

"Don't talk with your mouth full."

"Sorry."

"No, I didn't. Not exactly, but he came to my Oracle."

"At Delphi?"

"At Delphi. The Oracle told him what he would do." Or gave him hints, at least. I always tried to be clear and to the point, but clergy just can't resist a bit of theater. "There was an old prophesy, older than me, that Zeus would be kicked off the throne by his son, born of Metis."

"Athene's mother?"

"Good, five points." We clinked our paper cups together, though being paper they didn't actually 'clink'. More of a 'tap,' really. "But Athene was their only child."

"Because Zeus killed Metis to avoid the prophesy."

"Sort of. Killing gods is complicated. A grandson served just as well in the end, though."

"Why did it have to be a son? Couldn't Athene have kicked him off the throne herself?"

"I suppose. She was always daddy's little girl, though."

Ann poured herself another. A moment of quiet passed before she kicked me.

"So how did it happen?" she asked. I began to quietly panic. I couldn't remember. Had I even been there? These were events which no tale or tradition had set down, which no words had made as immortal as we are. The Muses and myself had agreed to that, and even Dionysus made no stage play of the story. Without tradition I had only memory, and memory over thousands of years was a fickle thing.

It occurred to me that I shouldn't spend the effort now for no better reason than a mortal's curiosity. Silent, I stared at nothing, and only gradually noticed that my eye's choice of nothing were folds of dark clothing draped over the sleeping nun. The cloth barely moved as she breathed, and her breath was uneven, out of rhythm, spent as though she dreamed of running. I looked to Ann, who sat silent, watching me, and wondered if she ever imagined herself growing so old and how she might breathe, then.

"I remember him, with a dust-covered cloak and a walking stick and a still-uneven growth of beard. Zeus looked down with a gleam in sky-blue eyes."

She waited. I sipped at an empty cup for what must have been the third or fourth time, then reached for the bottle and found it equally empty. I put down the cup but kept the bottle, its cool glass more comfortable and solid than the dissolving, purple-stained paper had been.

"There were no portents of impending doom that day. I suppose that itself was a sign; something disruptive enough to send ripples into random assortments of things like tossed sticks and tea leaves is always happening, or about to happen. I couldn't see a plot to kill a king or an impending earthquake *anywhere,* though I knew, having seen my uncle just the day before, that there was indeed an earthquake brewing.

"This silence had me in a foul mood by the time I set foot in Olympus. A few of us were lounging in the halls while others carried out affairs of state. Zeus, Cloud-Gatherer, was listening to a messenger from Dyaus, who was the sky and weather god of India at the time. As Jung would have it this made the two of them the same person, but similarities of office didn't help them get along any better. The messenger, a minor wind, listed grievances of overlapping weather patterns while Zeus toyed listlessly with a thunderbolt. I remembered a time when he would have incinerated the creature by now. Instead the father of gods rested chin in hand, arm on the armrest of Kronos' old throne, and silently watched the messenger with those blue eyes of his. It was anyone's guess whether he heard a single word.

"The godling came, then. An upstart, a child in search of something to be god of. He stood before the throne, having shoved aside the indignant wind in order to do so. Zeus smiled, such a smile as none of us had seen in many years, and he roared as he leapt down from his seat."

"But why did they fight at all?"

"Because it was time. Because it is difficult to take the place of one's ancestors if they never grow old."

"I wonder how Athene felt about all of this."

"I've never asked. But she didn't set foot in Olympus that day, nor any day thereafter." Tried to sip from the bottle, but it was still empty. I remembered the smell of mortal sweat from off the godling, and how Zeus' hands were dirtied by the other's grime of long travel.

"At any rate, they fought. Arms and shoulders of equal size strained against each other. They stood, less fragile than the foundations beneath them, and a spiderweb of cracks spread across the marble floor under their heels. "They fought, and our halls shook, and the temples that were shadows of our halls shook with them. Various statues dedicated to us fell as we ourselves were thrown to the ground. The weather outside achieved such a state of confusion that cosmological deities the world over would be sending complaints for months to come.

"To Zeus went the first throw, and he laughed as the godling fell. To his grandson went the second, and then there was silence. Zeus fell on the third throw. There was no fourth.

"We watched the young one pause to catch his breath, doubled over, his hands clasped to his knees. The godling stood, finally, and looked to the empty throne. Then he picked up his cloak and his staff from where they had fallen and left, sparing not a single glance for his audience. We watched him go, we who had commanded every aspect of the world he knew.

"Athene's son went on to spread a few of his mother's ideas about law, become an Athenian king, and die a mortal. No member of my pantheon has known just what to do with themselves since." I stared at the window. Then at my reflection in the window, wine-weary but nowhere near sleep.

"Thank you for the story," she said. "I really should offer you something in return."

"Your wine and attention were payment enough." There was pity in her, and I wanted none of it. But then she moved to sit between me and the window, my source of distraction, and the tiny, flickering light by the window ledge caught on her collarbone and cast a shadow there.

This was even harder to ignore than food in France had been.

"I should warn you," said I, unmoving, "that the last girl I kissed turned into a tree."

"That was quite awhile ago, wasn't it?" She took the empty bottle and set it aside.

"Happens more often than you might think."

Ann smiled a smile of mischief. "I'll take my chances. It might even be worth it, for people to later wonder how a tree came to grow in a train compartment."

Mortality can be a very, very difficult habit to break. My hand reached up to brush that lock of hair back from her face, and a fingertip grazed the curve of her ear as I tucked it there. I resolved to pay no further mind to the unconscious nun. "You know, I still can't remember anything about mice."

"Hush," she said. Ω

William Alexander tells us he has published speculative stories in Zahir, The SiNK, *and* Seven Days, *delivered a lecture on Tolkien in Tom Shippey's company, and wears a ring of Damascus steel. It is said that sixteen million men are direct descendants of Genghis Khan, but he insists that he is not one of them.*

FAMILY BUSINESS

by Maurice Broaddus

illustrated by David Grilla

Nathan Bratton was always closing his eyes to something.

Though only 16 kilometers separated Montego Bay from Maroontown, an eternity passed in the dips and sharp turns of the hillside roads. He forced his eyes shut. He hoped to sleep — if God so chose to favor him — but mostly he didn't want to watch.

The taxi driver expertly (Nathan prayed it was expertly) wove along the road. With each heave or lurch of the car, Nathan's mind registered a flood of images. The taxi honked. Kids laughed and yelled. Branches whipped the car. Tires squealed as they skirted what Nathan knew was the edge of a steep drop off. The taxi honked. A passing car returned the honk. The din was like mating sheep being run over. Nathan opened his eyes for a moment.

A bus passed excruciatingly close at its own breakneck speed. He tugged at his seat belt. Again.

Nathan reconsidered his reasons for coming back to Jamaica, although that made it seem like he had a choice. Nathan's mom was born in Maroontown. She left when she was a teenager. She visited often, bringing Nathan with her. She wanted him to know where he came from even if he didn't. Jamaicans struck Nathan as a proud people, proud to the point of arrogance. They acted like their culture was superior to everyone else's, their ways made more sense, their history somehow richer. Those beliefs were shoved down Nathan's throat. He took it for granted, the foods, the stories, his heritage, until his mom died last year. Only then did he realize how little he knew about her. And himself. He was a tabula rasa, part of his identity was missing. He'd planned, or meant to plan, a pilgrimage to Jamaica. Then yesterday the phone rang with news of his grandfather's death. This morning Nathan found himself on a plane bound for Jamaica. And as much as an outsider as he felt, he knew he had no choice but to come.

He was summoned.

"How much?" Nathan asked, tugging his suitcase free of the car seat.

"Five hundred dollars." The driver's thick accent clubbed his ears. Nathan watched as the driver studied him in his rear view mirror. Even with the $40 Jamaican for $1 U.S. exchange rate, the price seemed high. Nathan hated to haggle, but the word 'tourist' might as well have been spray painted across his forehead.

"You must be mad," Nathan said, believing that the key to effective haggling was in the attitude. "That doesn't even sound right."

"Five hundred dollars," the driver repeated.

Nathan spied a familiar face pulling alongside the taxi. He removed a folded photograph from his vest pocket. A wedding photo of his mother's sister Karen and her new husband. The photograph was little more than a month old. "You must be Uncle Edward."

Edward filled his police Jeep with his massive build. He opened the door and put one freshly polished black boot on the ground as he waited for the transaction to finish. Stiffly pressed Navy slacks with two red stripes running down the side and an equally pressed light blue shirt was the uniform of a ranking police officer. A sense of menace exuded from Edward like a sinister shadow. Staring into his black eyes was like being raked by shards of glass. The taxi driver locked eyes with him momentarily. Edward nodded.

"I'm sorry. How much was that ride?" Nathan repeated.

"Fifty dollars." the driver muttered. He gripped his steering wheel like a drowning man to his life preserver. "Respec', corporal."

"Respect, man," Edward dismissed the driver. He looked about conspicuously, then pulled his black cap curtly to the front of his head. He approached Nathan in arrogant strides. Though Edward's hands were soft and manicured, there was a heaviness to his handshake.

"It's good to finally meet you, Uncle Edward."

"It's good to meet some of Karen's American

family." Edward's words rang with exaggerated enunciation, as if speaking slowly for Nathan's benefit. It was only mildly condescending and was better than the sing-songy, frenetic accent that sounded like it could have been as easily Chinese as English.

"I'm happy to hear someone I actually understand." Nathan said.

"Oh, surprised to hear my command of the English language?" Edward's voice bubbled with a self-satisfied haughtiness. Nathan was swept along in the intimidating charm of Edward's serpentine grin.

"I didn't mean any offense."

"None taken. Not everyone speaks in ignorant patois." Edward gestured toward his Jeep. Nathan quickly learned to hate the silence. Edward spoke in a loop, as if he had rehearsed only a certain amount of topics. Any lull in conversation was filled with Edward re-capping how important he was. As senior Justice of the Peace for his ward, he knew everyone. He was well traveled. He'd been to America, England, and Canada and had no trouble driving on either side of the road. His authority was such that he could have anyone jailed, for no reason, for three months. Nathan listened amiably, a forced smile plastered across his face.

Edward droned on, in love with the sound of his own voice. Either that or he was simply used to people hanging on his every word. Every so often, Nathan caught Edward glancing at him, trying to read him. Nathan smiled, continuing the dance of first impressions. The radio distracted him with jingles for Prima milk. IRIE FM was the main station received in the country. The trip took a surreal turn as a reggae version of "We are the Champions" played.

"How much longer to your house?" Nathan masked the impatience in his voice as travel fatigue.

"It's just around the corner," Edward chuckled to himself. "Everything's 'just around the corner' out here. You can go 10 miles around that 'corner' and still not be there. But if I honk my horn from here, they'll have the gate open by the time we get there. Supper will be ready."

"By the way, thanks for letting me stay here."

"No problem. Family takes care of family."

"I'm full." Nathan pushed his plate to the side. His palate, too weak for ackee and saltfish, felt fairly safe picking at the curried goat, boiled bananas, and yams. The food sat in his full stomach. The heavy bass of Beenie Man's "Betta Learn" thumped from down the street. Many people slowly gathered for the funeral though it was not until tomorrow. The gerriae, which Nathan likened to an Irish wake, started the day of his grandfather's death. The music, dancing and food would not stop until his burial. Friends and family were flying or driving in from all over, though no one else dared ask to stay with Edward.

"Before you make good food go to waste, 'mek belly bust.' "

Edward scraped the untouched ackee and saltfish onto his plate.

"Aunt Karen always did cook enough for an army. I guess she had to, I mean, granddad did have 37 children."

"You mean 36." Angela said. Angela McGhie was Aunt Karen's daughter from her first marriage. Nathan and Angela bonded immediately since they were both in their early twenties. Her mocha complexion only deepened the melancholy that girded her face. Long braids of thick black hair framed her oval face. She possessed a hustler's eyes and a rogue's heart, but everyone in the family had a bit of The Scoudrel in them.

"No, 37. Here's the notice." Nathan fished in his briefcase, past a flurry of Post-It notes and scraps of paper, to reveal a folder. Most of what he knew about his grandfather he learned in the obituary column. "See here, he was survived by 37 children, 139 grandchildren, and 3 great grandchildren."

"Yeh," Angela paused meditatively, the names ticking off in her head, "We forget 'bout Hubert. He was a baby when he died."

"Yeah, crib death. I heard." Nathan attempted to wrap his mind around the idea of 139 grandchildren.

"Hmph." Angela's fork clattered noisily against her near empty plate. They sat around the table as Aunt Karen fussed in the kitchen. Edward's son, Saul, quietly ate. Nathan watched as Saul surreptitiously dropped a piece of meat for one of the dogs to eat. The other dogs perked up with interest.

"What are your dogs' names?" Nathan asked.

"Names?" Saul asked.

"Don't they have names?"

"No suh. We call 'im puppy an' 'im come. We call dat one puppy, an' 'im come."

"Who name dem dogs?" Angela interjected. "Dat's like fe name your chickens."

"But we eat our chickens." Nathan said. "They don't run around the yard."

"We 'ave our dogs jus' fe mek noise at night. Fe

tiefs."

"He nuh 'ave dogs in America?" Saul asked.

"Yeh, but dey 'ave dem all in dey bed wid dem."

"It's time for bed," Edward cut short the conversation.

"Come on," Angela reached for Saul's hand. "I'll tell you a story."

"Can I listen?" Nathan asked.

"Come on."

Angela told Saul the story of Bra Ananse saving Bra Buffu from Bra Snake by tricking Bra Snake into his own trap. Nathan listened intently, jotting down the story onto one of his Post-It notes. "An' he and Bra Buffu went off fe de village," Angela concluded, "leaving Bra Snake for de wood cutter's axe."

Saul grinned broadly, then rolled over. She leaned forward and kissed him. She ran her fingers softly through his hair.

"Was there a moral to that story?" Nathan whispered.

"Poppa seh, 'de same knife wha stick sheep, stick goat,' " she said, looking down at the soundly sleeping Saul. "Why you interested in stories?"

"My mother used to tell me the same stories when I was growing up. Over and over. Oh, man they got on my nerves. Then, when I grew older, I realized I had no stories to tell. I miss them, especially the duppy stories."

"Duppies dead out."

"Ghosts don't die out," Nathan said.

"People don' believe in dem. Dey nuh scared of dem."

"That's because there are more frightening evils among the living."

Nathan tossed fitfully in his bed. Aunt Karen placed bottles of Jamaican Rum Creme on the dresser, in case Nathan wanted a midnight nip. A curtain-less window opened against the night heat, allowing shadows of the burglar bars to play along the far wall. Several mosquitos buzzed too close to his ears. Nathan flung the sweat soaked sheets to the other side of the bed. He prayed that sheer exhaustion would carry him to sleep. The wind murmured its dirge through the banana trees. The wind-whipped leaves produced a sound easily mistaken for rainfall.

The dogs growled. Again. The snarls usually signaled a dispute over sleeping arrangements that ended in yelping. This time was different. The tenor had changed. Nathan grabbed a bottle of Rum Creme and headed outdoors. It tasted like a vanilla milkshake spiked with rum, albeit 200 proof rum. The house was an anomaly along the street side. Their neighbors dwelt in little more than tin-roofed shanties. Edward's home hid from the road behind a grand concrete wall, ornately decorated with roaring lions. Iron gates enclosed the veranda. Even Nathan heard the rumors of how crookedness swirled around Edward like an inescapable odor, but he dismissed them as the gossip that generally accompanied all Jamaican police. Nathan circled around the house, enjoying the night air outside of his stifling room. Hundreds of stars flecked the night sky, freed from the cloak of pollution. The crickets hummed like overhead power lines, interrupted by the occasional cry of "ka-ka" of passing birds. As Nathan approached the side of the house, the dogs whined, as if disturbed, then abruptly stopped. Fear fluttered briefly in his chest, like a vulture disturbed from its perch. Nathan heeded that primitive part of his brain sensitive to danger, though he overrode the urge to flee as he pressed himself against the house wall. He peered around the corner, only to see the dogs sitting in a perfect semi-circle. Their attention seemed engaged on someone in the middle, engulfed in the shadows of the trees. The unseen presence charged the air around him. Nathan gulped courage from his bottle.

The figure defied recognition from so far away, so Nathan crouched alongside the wall and edged closer. Hidden behind the rain-water barrels, Nathan chanced another glance. The shadow-enshrouded man reached out toward the dogs, mimicking a petting motion. The dogs wagged their tails merrily. The wind died, an eerie stillness settling on the scene. Faint traces of marijuana smoke emanated from the neighbor's home. The gerriae revelers had long turned in for the night, readying themselves for the funeral tomorrow. No traffic rumbled along the street. Nathan fumbled with his bottle as he neared the distracted dogs. Each footstep firmly set itself along the pebble-strewn path. The figure's haunted face was familiar to Nathan, though he only recognized it from a yellowed photo crammed into his bedroom mirror like a mute guardian: a younger version of Nathan's grandfather. The essence of his grandfather flickered in the gentle eyes eclipsed within the hardness of his face. Except that the figure stood taller than Nathan recalled. Too much taller.

He hovered above the ground.

Nathan dropped his bottle. The shattering glass splintered the silence. The man's eyes bored into Nathan. The figure melted into the night as if a spell had been broken, little more than a memory captured from a fleeting dream. Nathan's hand grappled for anything to steady him. The Rum Cremes must've been more potent than he thought.

"Don't sit there. That's Poppa's chair," Aunt Karen said. Nathan froze in mid-sit down, not sure if she was serious. She patted a nearby chair. "Sit down over here."

"Uh, okay," Nathan tried to keep an open mind. He wasn't conceited enough to consider himself sophisticated, but his mind often wondered whether or not his people were backward. It was bad enough that they spent the morning of the funeral fretting about the house. Death was little more than a chore that needed to be attended to. Aunt Karen shuffled outside to collect the laundry from the line.

That unnerved him more than any foolish superstition. "But why save his seat for him. He's probably not going to need it again."

"Oh, but he might," she huffed over the basket. Nathan ran over to grab it, but Aunt Karen brushed him aside with her don't-make-me-box-you-over look. "He was a powerful obeah man,"

"What do you mean?"

"Me seh he worked obeah, set duppies," Aunt Karen said as she folded the laundry. "True, true. 'Is people dey come trouble 'im, all vex up 'bout dem neighbor or someting'. He work obeah on 'em, an' seldom asked fe anyting."

"Really? Interesting."

"You an obeah man, too," Aunt Karen said. "Yes suh, you 'ave faith, so if an obeah man tried to work obeah on you, it wouldn't work."

"So if you believe in it, it works on you. If you don't, it won't."

"Mostly people wit grudges seek out obeah men. Some obeah are real," Angela interrupted from the doorway. She cut a sensual figure, even in her mourning outfit. Nathan rose, taking his cue to leave. *Most* are con men. Li'l more than thugs. If they say someting bad will 'appen, dey may do it demselves."

"How can you tell a real obeah man," Nathan asked. Angela led the way as they walked along the gravel path that headed toward the church. It was a short walk cutting through the property.

"Real obeah men seldom look you in a de eye. Dey carry a basket or whatever dat 'olds 'is tings.

Dey of'en wear a red flannel shirt or someting. He 'as fe kill a member of his own family as the final rite to become a true obeah man."

"You ever been to one?" Nathan asked Angela.

"Once. 'Im read me up."

"Told you your future?"

"Yeh. 'e tell me, me not gon keep no work unless me let 'im give me a guard ring. So me ask 'im, 'How much is de guard ring gon cost.'

" 'Im say, '$8000.' " She bugged her eyes out in mock amazement.

" 'Je-sus,' me seh, 'me no 'ave no $8000 fe pay you.'

" 'Im say me fe give 'im $4000 as downpayment. If not, 'im seh me gwon dead in a two week time."

"So what happened?"

"Me no know. That was three weeks ago." Her laugh was as free and easy as it was infectious. Her laugh trailed to silence when she glimpsed Edward sauntering toward the church. A somber pall settled between them. She whispered as he passed. "Do you ever wonder 'bout Edward?"

"Wonder what?" Nathan asked.

"Sometimes me tink he did someting to Poppa." Angela cast her eyes downward, as if not wanting them to betray her to Edward. "Death's shadow is 'pon 'is face. You no see it?"

"What? Obeah?" Nathan smirked, thinking himself cuter than he was. Angela was less than amused.

"Shh. Ne'er mind. The funeral soon start."

They made their way to the front of the church. Everyone stood as the coffin was brought up the steep rocky steps to the church. A grey shroud covered the coffin. Once the coffin rested before the pulpit, the casket lid was opened so that Poppa was visible during the sermon. His appearance was waxy, even dehydrated. Rumors circulated all week as to the cause of his death. Some said he only had diarrhea but was too embarrassed to tell anyone. Some said he was poisoned. Some said a rival obeah man worked powerful obeah on him. He seemed so small, almost lost in the silken linens of the casket.

The church filled to standing room only. The doors in the back of the building were opened so that the overflow crowd could catch a glimpse (and be seen). It was quite a spectacle. Poppa was a retired district constable, so many off-duty Montego Bay policemen lined the walls, decked in full regalia. People were there from all over Maroontown, even as far as Garlands. Angela explained to Nathan that it was because of more rumors. Word spread that the will had been revised to divide the farm among the family. That rang true to Nathan: when his mother visited, she brought all manner of goods and merchandise from America and left all that she brought, even her own clothes and luggage. "Family took care of family," she said.

When it was time, a Rastafarian — with a huge nest of dreadlocks tucked under his multi-colored hat — crawled into the sepulcher to receive the coffin. Whispers churned among the gathering, since only family was allowed to gather immediately around the sepulcher. And Rastafarians never went near the dead.

"Nathan, I think it's time we talked. Man-to-man," Edward beamed with malevolent intensity. Angela shook her head 'no.' An uneasy chill stirred in Nathan's gut.

"Sure, Uncle Edward."

The night was unusually frigid as a wind sliced through the lush hills. Brooding clouds encroached the baleful eye of the moon. A distant rumble disquieted the sky. Suspense reduced Nathan to halting breaths.

"What were you and your cousin whispering about this morning?"

"Oh that?" Nathan was tempted to breath a sigh of relief. "Nothing. She was telling me tales of obeah men. Do you believe in that stuff?"

"I don't have time for that necromancy foolishness."

"Why do you ask?" Nathan still waited to exhale.

"I just didn't want you meddling in my family's business."

"Our." The word leapt from Nathan's mouth before he could stop it.

"What?"

"*Our* family's business." Nathan heard his voice, though his mind wanted his mouth to shut up. Words kept tripping from his tongue. "We are in the same family now."

"Let me ask you something," Edward half-smiled as if enjoying some game. He reached to his side and unsnapped his holster. "Have you ever fired a gun?"

"No." Nathan eyed the holstered gun. His armpits itched ferociously. A nervous perspiration dampened his forehead. His mind raced, mapping possible escape routes. All of a sudden, Nathan counted all of his dumb mistakes. He let himself be convinced to meet this virtual stranger alone. He didn't bring a weapon with him. Nathan's

eyes followed as Edward drew the gun in mock-gunslinger style. Nathan flinched, but remained rooted.

"Take it. Go on."

"Okay." Nathan held the gun with the tips of his fingers.

"How does it feel?"

"Heavy."

"How does it make you feel?"

"What do you mean?" Nathan asked.

"I'll show you. Feel the gun in your hands. Aim it over there." Edward pointed to a distant hill. He spoke slowly, almost seductively. No lights glimmered along the valley. "Pull the trigger."

The gun cracked with deadly authority, jerking in Nathan's hands. Nathan's ears rang as the discharge was louder than Nathan imagined it would be. An acrid odor, like burnt ozone, assaulted his nostrils. He held the gun where he fired. Nathan didn't know what lesson he was suppose to glean from this exhibition. Edward continued his baiting smile.

"It's about control." Edward grabbed the gun at the barrel and turned it, and Nathan, towards him. "Right now, you hold my life in your hands."

"I don't think . . ."

"How does it make you feel?" Edward's eyes burned with a devil's luster. He wetted his lips. Nathan was unnerved enough to begin trembling. His stomach churned with imminent queasiness. He could only stare along the sights. He itched with mosquito bites that he didn't remember getting. His palms slickened against the grip. Edward reached for the gun. He removed it from Nathan's grasp. Nathan's hands still cupped the air, not daring to move. "Control. Power. No fear. Don't cross me."

Just then, a sound pealed in the distance. Like a thunderous snort. Rain poured from the skies hitting the corrugated tin canopy next door with such fury it resonated with the roar of distant applause. Beneath the din was the sound of jangling metal getting nearer.

"What was that?"

"Nothing. Thunder. Let's go inside." Edward's voice wavered. It was slight and quickly covered up, but Nathan heard it and found it comforting.

A few moments later, another grunt bellowed, shaking the floor. Aunt Karen scurried to the living room and called from the window.

"G'wan fe bed," she ushered Nathan to his room, "an' don' look outside."

Nathan retreated to his room, not bothering to turn on any lights. Outside the window was a terrible tramping, as if some behemoth trudged along the banana groves. It occurred to Nathan to peek outside, but his aunt's warnings echoed in his head with the urgency of angels to Lot's wife. The clanking sounds of metal coalesced into something familiar. Like chains. It sounded like something bowled over the banana trees and ate the gungoo pea stalks.

With each hideous snort, the house warmed up like a make-shift furnace. Nathan sat on the corner of his bed wondering if this was some sort of Jamaican fire drill. He had come to Jamaica to answer one nagging question: who am I? Yet all he had seen left him no closer to any real answer. The figure and the dogs. Angela. Duppies. The funeral. Edward. The gun. Obeah. If a destiny awaited him, it had to come to him.

The chains rattled outside his doorstep before fading into the night.

Last night seemed like a nightmare induced by a bad batch of goat belly soup. No damage had been done to the groves. He woke to the usual bleating of goats, though the dogs were no where to be found. He found Angela washed blood from the house walls with a casualness that stupefied him. The blood was smeared, almost sprayed. A garish display that felt more like a warning than anything else.

"Look how de duppy kiss me last night," Angela laughted as she pointed to a bruise on her arm.

"Oh, really?" Nathan asked, unsure if she was even joking.

"Shut yo' face gal wit dat nonsense," Edward scolded. He seemed more on edge than ever. He glanced at Nathan and regained his composure. And his unaffected speech. "I'm sure our guest doesn't wish to hear such . . . foolishness."

"Me love fe chat, it don't mean nuting'."

"You love chat too much," Aunt Karen yelled from the porch. " 'Ere comes Saul. Mek 'im put on 'is school clothes."

Aunt Karen, often lamented that none of the current generation wanted to farm. It was, after all, the family business. So Saul had to work in the field before he went to school. The banana exports were due soon. Saul headed straight to the house from the field. What was once Sunday dress pants was worn to feather-thin, dirt-encrusted fringe. His tennis shoes were barely soled and his New York Knicks jersey was soiled to inscrutability. He brandished a machete that was over half his size. Angela followed him into his room to hurry him. Nathan trailed behind her.

"Alright, what was that last night?" Nathan asked.

"You mean de rollin' calf?" Saul giggled. "Aunt Karen tol' me de tale las' night."

"A what?"

"You *did* wan' a duppy story," Angela said. "It obeah man duppy."

"It come 'roun' between Christmas an' New Year's," Saul called out from the bathroom. "It a huge someting wid chains 'roun' 'is neck an' fire in a dem eye. You can't look in a dem eye. It's breath kill you dead. He can't trouble you on de straight road or in shadow of a tree. Otherwise . . ."

"Anyting dem meet in a dem way, dem kill." Angela finished.

"Bye, uncle," Saul threw his backpack over his neatly pressed khaki colored school uniform. Nathan silently thrilled at the respect shown by being called uncle. Saul shook his hand with a fearful trembling, like he wanted to warn him. He looked over his shoulder, toward the door, and thought better of it. Angela grabbed Nathan's hand, escorting him along, leading him back to the kitchen.

"You are quite fortunate to marry a man like me." Edward said, noting Nathan and Angela's return. "You are lucky to have a man who has breakfast cooked by the time you get home."

"Me know, me know," Aunt Karen said.

"Now I cleaned up the kitchen when I cooked. I expect it to stay that way."

Edward raised his hand, only to pat her shoulder, but she shrank back, like an oft-scolded dog. He headed toward his bedroom. Aunt Karen ate her breakfast in solitude. Angela waited a few minutes then gestured for Nathan to follow, leading him down the porch steps behind the house. She stopped below Edward's balcony. Angela cocked her ears toward the opened window.

"What're you doing?" Nathan asked.

"Shh."

Edward's distinctive baritone echoed as he spoke on the phone.

"Yeh man, the property's practically mine . . . banana farm too . . . I know . . . she got it all . . . he never had a chance to change his will . . . sure she'll sign it over to me . . . interest of British importers . . . not often an opportunity like this comes along." Edward loosed a chilling chortle, its echoes scraped across their souls like gnarled fingernails.

Nathan lacked Angela's surefootedness; he stumbled over the jutting stones of the house base. Edward awaited them on the veranda. He dropped a basket of laundry, apparently for Angela to hang.

"Nathan, you'll never fin' a woman if you keep 'round your cousin. You carry on like a couple in love. You two are aware you're family."

"That never stopped you," her words, slicing like daggers through her teeth, as she turned to pick up the basket. Nathan's heart stopped in his chest. Silence reigned for an interminable span of seconds. Edward shifted noisily before turning sharply on his heel. His voice was a tyrannical rumble, like crashing waves.

"Don't poke around my business."

Nathan sat along the beach edge, fascinated by the water's clarity. He stamped his foot underwater just to watch the sand stir about then settle. His hands dug nervous holes in the sand next to him. Storm clouds gripped the hills of Maroontown in a terrible grasp; a view best appreciated from Brighton Beach. Vestigial winds whipped sand particles across his back like a stern taskmaster. Angela delighted in Nathan's suggestion to visit the beach. He found it difficult to watch Angela in her own element. She enjoyed the liveliness of the beach. Her playfully flirtatious manner made her quite popular, however, she quickly tired of the attentions of the crowd. Nathan felt relieved to see her walk toward him. Despite her joviality, Angela carried herself with a melancholy air, a profound sadness that saturated her every movement. The only time it didn't haunt her was when she played with children. Even then, the sadness transformed only to a longing. Maybe that was why Nathan felt so protective of her. She was at once fragile and hardened. Angela sat close to him. They watched the events of the beach, like it was their personal stage. Two young boys, not quite teenagers, shadowed a tourist who might as well worn an 'I'm a tourist, please rob me' shirt rather than his orange and turquoise flower print shirt.

"See those two pick'ney behind dat white man?"

"Yeah?"

"They're pick pockets."

Closer to them, a Rasta performed his own show for three college frat boys giving them a "Jamaican Experience" to tell the folks back home about. He sang for awhile, breaking his routine to sit for conversation. He borrowed one of their Walkmans to provide extemporaneous commentary on their music. One of the frat boys sat up in attention, extremely entertained.

"'E betta be careful," she said. "'Im tek 'is time moving further and further away as he dances. Soon he take off wid it."

"Ain't that the same Rasta who pulled Poppa's coffin into the sepulcher?"

"Yeh, dat's Bigga. He didn't even go fe 'is own mother's funeral. Dreads seh, 'when dey dead, dey dead.' Won' have anyting fe do wid dead bodies."

"Why not?"

"Dead bodies are unclean. Like pigs."

"They don't eat pork either?"

"No suh. You give 'im a box o' animal crackers, he'd even pick out de pigs befo' he ate dem."

Bigga noticed their laughter. His scruffy blue jean shorts, along with his red-yellow-green crocheted hat, flapped as he danced next to his knapsack. He sang along with whatever melody overtook him, occasionally casting a sideways glance toward the prying eyes of Nathan and Angela. One of the men got up for a drink run. He brought back four bottles of Guinness: one for him and each of his friends, and one for his dreadlocked acquaintance. A few minutes later, Bigga wandered toward Angela and Nathan, neither of whom hid their nosiness.

"Irie."

"Irie, dread." Angela said

"Why you watch me so close?"

"Just watching you entertain folks." Nathan said

"Wha', you wan' be like this Rasta?"

"Yeh, Rasta," Angela mocked, "jus' like you, some mawga foot dread. Move yo'self, you too facety."

"You wicked, gal," Bigga turned to Nathan. "No suh, what you need is fe eat a plate of steamfish, drink two Guiness, and smoke two spliffs. Thas how you 'andle a big gal like this'un. You do dat, and you break a woman six times before you break once." Nathan and Angela looked at each other and burst into titters. Bigga took another spiteful swig of his Guinness.

"I'll have to remember that." Nathan finally said. "Too bad you don't know anything about obeah."

"Obeah. It jus' science," Bigga nonchalantly said, knowing eyes peering over his tipping beer bottle.

"What, you an obeah man, too? Like my grand-dad?"

"You wan' me fe read you up?"

"Yeah," Nathan offered Bigga his pen. Bigga fitfully wrapped his hands around it and closed his eyes. His face contorted with some unseen agony. He winced, tilting his head to the side. To Nathan, it seemed quite the performance, but his skepticism gave way to apprehension. Feigned or not, Bigga's apparent fretfulness caused anxiety to creep into Nathan. Angela stared with equal, but silent fascination. Bigga set the pen down and foraged in his knapsack. Overturning various accouterments — feathers, beaks, horns, bones, hair, dried herbs, balls of clay bound with twine — he decided on a small ball, little bigger than a clear marble. Nathan's rising anxiety returned to cool skepticism.

"I look in a it fe see who trouble you," a fearful grimace of confirmation soon flickered on his face. "Here, take this. This will help protect you."

Bigga tied a tiny leather pouch around Nathan's neck. Nathan often watched his life play out like he was little more than a spectator. Of all the things to happen on this trip, this was the first to feel natural. The pouch necklace felt right. He asked the only question he was capable of mustering at this point. "How much?"

"Nutting," Bigga said sharply. "You 'ave potential. Only need ta be taught. Keep it, man. It's a gift."

That evening, Nathan found his suitcase perched on his bed, spilling its contents like a disemboweled stomach. The papers of his briefcase were scattered across the room. All of his belongings had been thoroughly rummaged.

"Where's Edward, Aunt Karen?" Nathan demanded.

"Whas de matta, boy," she flustered, "he went out fe visit Poppa's grave. Him vex 'bout someting."

Nathan stormed toward the door, until Angela blocked his way.

"You can't go. Thas what he wan' you fe do. Meet on 'is terms."

"Well, I wouldn't want to disappoint him, now would I?"

"You no easy, cho," she sucked her teeth disgustedly at him, a habit that never ceased to annoy him. He glared at her, but she turned her head from him. So he left. He voice echoed after him. "Lord Jesus, he no easy."

The family cemetery was not far behind Ed-ward's home, half way down a hill that leveled to a plateau. Rocks spit dust into the night air marking his passage. The overcast moon scowled. Nathan paused at the stone marker of his grandfather's tomb. Edward stood calmly on the other side of the small cemetery, with his back turned toward Nathan.

"I still know what you did, even if I don't have any proof. You know as well as I do, Jamaicans, especially Jamaican police, aren't real fussy about proof," Nathan shouted.

"Did what?" Edward asked. He turned, revealing a joyless smile as he slowly walked toward Nathan.

"Kill Poppa," Nathan's voice softened. He wasn't sure at what point his grandfather became "Poppa" to him. Edward stepped closer.

"I don't know what you're talking about." Menace laced Edward's calm measured words. Nathan took a few steps backwards.

"I bet you don't. I won't stop, you know. The will can be contested. Better yet, Aunt Karen wouldn't sign anything over to someone she suspects killed her father."

"You haven't learned anything have you? You're in my country. My town. Your laws do not apply. Here, my will is done." Edward's hand patted against his side, toying with whatever hung there. "It's a shame that I couldn't find you sooner."

"Sooner?"

" 'You hear how your people dem behave? Those rasclots from de shop got a hold of you. It was all I could do fe chase dem after dey tief you.' " Edward mimicked the gossip he would spread. "If only you hadn't been so determined to come on your own. I, for one, was greatly saddened. Family is supposed to *take care* of family."

Edward pulled his machete from its scabbard, the dim moonlight glinting off its razor-edged blade. He stood between Nathan and the road, blocking the path. Nathan dashed into the banana tree grove. The leaves cut into Nathan's soft flesh as he ran. Still in beach attire, he cursed himself for not dressing more properly. The sand in his clothes scraped as he ran, rubbing his skin raw. The wind ripped through the leaves, creating the illusory sound of a deluge. Nathan stumbled blindly through the trees. Edward stalked close behind him, slower, but with sure footfalls, like a man who knew the grove like the back of his hand. A truck banged loudly along the road behind him. Above him. Beside him. He didn't know. He felt the truck rumble past as if his own stomach suddenly grumbled. Nathan's breath grew ragged quickly. The trees thinned ahead. Nathan hoped that was because they led to the back of the house.

The trees opened into an isolated clearing.

Wan moonlight weakly lit the area. Nathan's arms swung wildly as he ground to a halt. As he regained his bearings, he realized that the house was at the top of the next hill over. He swallowed deeply, his breathing little more than short, dry rasps. Nathan heard a tuneless whistle from behind him. Edward gripped the machete's taped handle firmly, tantalizingly slicing the air in front of him. He feinted to one side, letting Nathan flinch impotently, for the sheer joy of extending his game. Nathan's exposed skin rippled with gooseflesh. Nausea pooled in his belly, threatening to overwhelm him. The hair on the back of his neck stood up as if he had backed into a socket. Edward halted and looked around. He felt it too. Something approached.

The shadows stirred nearby. A forlorn wail erupted all about the trees. Birds fluttered. All else seemed to fall silent. A harsh grating echoed closer, like a train braking in the woods. Edward craned his neck from side to side. The clanging of huge chains dragged in the distance. Nathan felt the blood in his veins freeze with terror. A foul, dank odor seared his nostrils. It accompanied the nearing cacophony of a maelstrom of metal.

A shape slowly materialized into view.

Twin red pyres peered through the night. The abomination was twice the size of a bull. It was mostly black, with white patches, approximating the shape of a hornless goat. It had no mouth. A collar strained against its thick neck, attached to a series of chains that dragged along the ground. One of its front feet looked like a horse's hoof; the other, a human foot. Its back legs were reminiscent of goat legs. A cow-like tail swooshed broadly over its back. The raw stench of wet fur gagged both Nathan and Edward. The grotesquerie seemed to have absorbed all manner of life in its travels.

The rolling calf galloped faster than any living horse. Nathan simply fell and scampered backwards as fast as he could away from the horror. Nathan shrank away, hiding in the shadows, praying it wouldn't notice him. He watched in horror as the creature chased down Edward, and cornered him. Edward swung his machete haphazardly at it, for all the good it did him. The rolling calf pinned Edward with its front legs. The horse

hoof planted squarely in Edward's gut, the human foot pressed against his neck. It had no mouth, but it bent its face low toward Edward. Whatever awful exhalations it expelled choked Edward. Nathan saw the comically quizzical expression on Edward's face as his skin shriveled, as if his insides had been sucked dry. Even as he closed his eyes, Nathan still heard the snapping, the rending, the sounds of . . . breaking. Then the dull thud of a machete hitting the ground. When he opened his eyes, Edward had vanished without a trace.

The rolling calf turned toward Nathan.

Nathan cringed against a tree, his arms thrown up, waiting for the inevitable to play itself out. The rolling calf snorted its dreadful cough. Nathan's mouth dried, as if hot sand filled it. His throat closed as a scream died on his lips. Each desperate gasp pained his chest. His muscles convulsed into seizing knots. The howl of the wind fluttered the banana trees creating their rain-like patter. The rolling calf stopped just short of him. Its flame-socketed eyes locked onto Nathan's primitive pendant. It exhaled with a frustrated humphing of a donkey's bray as if it were reminded of something. The whole area grew hot with each breath, its snorts exuding blue flames, far more hot than the tiny flames should've produced. The rolling calf fixed its gaze toward Nathan. He peeked from behind his shielding arms. He saw something familiar, like the essence of country geniality hidden among the horror.

Nathan closed his eyes. He waited for the pain that never came. When he chanced opening his eyes, he found himself alone. Except for the red scarf that lay at his feet. That was when he knew: the farm had to be worked, but obeah was the true family business. And it was his turn to run it. Ω

Maurice Broaddus works as an environmental toxicologist by day and a horror writer by night. The present story won first place for long fiction in the story contest sponsored by the World Horror Convention in 2003 and judged by the editors of Weird Tales.

The Classic Horrors

It took her a moment prolonged as a nightmare to realize that it had been crushed between lift and shaft—for as the doors struggled open, the face began to tear.
Down There by Ramsey Campbell

by Allen Koszowski

TO GRANDMOTHER'S HOUSE

Nina Kiriki Hoffman

"Why do I always have to sleep with Grandma?" I asked from the back seat of the station wagon.

My older brother Brian, thirteen, sitting in the middle with his knees high because his feet were on the hump, jabbed me in the ribs with his elbow. Beyond Brian, my oldest brother Russell groaned and looked out the window. Something had happened to Russell since Halloween. He was suddenly Too Old to put up with me and Brian, even though he was only fifteen. Everything we did irritated him, which just made me more determined to make him stop being Too Old. I hadn't figured out how yet. Too Old was a very effective tactic.

Mom turned around in the front passenger seat and glared at me. "Because you're the girl, Lacey. Why do you always ask that question when you already know the answer?"

I jabbed Brian back and thought of my knitting needles, but Mom had made me put them in my luggage. Knitting while I was in a car made me carsick. Almost everything made me carsick or gave me nightmares. That was me, Carsick and Nightmare Girl. Everybody was tired of me having these problems, so I'd learned to stop talking about them, but Mom could still tell when I was carsick, because I threw up. She stopped me from doing anything she had identified that would make me sick. So I was just going to have to live with Brian bruises. He was bigger and could jab a lot harder than I could.

"What's so bad about sleeping with Grandma?" Dad asked.

"She smells. She snores. She hates me."

"Oh, come on, Lacey, she doesn't hate you. She loves you."

"No, Dad," said Russell in his new, long-suffering, reasonable grownup voice, "Grandma hates all of us."

Dad turned to look at us, and Mom yelled for him to keep his eyes on the road. We almost hit a pickup truck, but Dad swerved in time, so, of course, eventually, like, two hours later, we ended up at Grandma's house.

Grandma answered the door after Dad bingbonged. She was thin and sharp-edged — it hurt to hug her. She had deep cheeks and pepper-and-salt gray hair cut short. She wore a red dress with a white polka-dot collar and looked like an ancient cowgirl waxwork someone had dressed up against its will.

She smiled. "Hello! Hello! Welcome, everyone! Merry Christmas Eve! Come in, come in. Put those presents under the tree, children, and come and have some of my special holiday eggnog!"

The house smelled good: pine from the decorated branch on the bookshelves, just-baked cookie smell from the kitchen. Brian and Russ and I took the presents into the living room and stowed them under the tree.

This year's tree was white and gold. The tree was flocked solid white and shedding little flakes of tree dandruff on the pale green carpet, and it was hung with nothing but golden balls, oh, yeah, and white lights. It was a two-note symphony of color.

"Oh, joy," said Russell.

Brian raided the candy dish. "Peppermints and chocolate kisses," he reported. After he stuck a peppermint in his mouth, he poured the rest of the candy into his pocket. Two kisses fell on the floor.

"I dibs the dish in Grandma's room," I said.

"Not if I get there first," Brian yelled, and ran off. Like he had more room in his pockets? He just wanted to get everything before I could.

"Children," said Russell. But he grabbed the two kisses Brian had dropped, leaving me without any candy.

I hate being the youngest.

"Brian! Russell! Lacey! Help unload the car!" Dad yelled.

We were only staying at Grandma's overnight, but it always turned into this huge production, because we had our Christmas morning over here, which included all the presents, plus for Christmas Eve we had special dress-up clothes, different from the ones we wore to drive over here in, and different from the pajamas we'd be wearing when we opened presents tomorrow.

This was the third year we'd done Grandma Christmas. We started it after Grandpa died. Mom thought Grandma was lonely. I figured Grandma was almost resigned to Grandma Christmas, but wished it would go away. Mom and Grandma never seemed to be able to figure out what the other one really wanted, though they'd known each other all Mom's life.

Russ and I went back for more armloads of presents. I saw several intriguing presents with my name on them and started to feel better. So what if Grandma hated me and I had to sleep with her? There were still presents!

While I was looking at the presents I was carrying, I bumped into one of the little tables Grandma had scattered around the living room, and knocked off a statue of a shepherd boy. His head broke off. I tossed the presents under the tree and went back to pick up the boy, to see if I could stick him back together and pretend nothing had happened. Grandma came in when I had his body in one hand and his head in the other.

"That was my mother's," she whispered.

"I'm sorry," I said. "I'm sorry, Grandma. It was an accident. I'm sorry."

She took the pieces of boy away from me, mumbling something about SuperGlue.

When we'd unpacked the car, Grandma gave us eggnog and cookies. Even though she looked like an antique cowgirl, Grandma could cook. The cookies were great. This year the eggnog tasted strange, though. There was some new spice in it. At first I didn't like it. It tasted like perfume. Then I kind of got into it, and I had seconds and thirds. Grandma smiled at me as she poured.

Time slid away. We got dressed up for dinner, and Mom brushed my hair really hard, but I didn't say anything, even when she dressed it in sausage curls, which I hate. Dinner was a haze of candlelight; good food; and Mom, Dad, and Grandma having a lot of hilarious conversation and reminiscences while Brian, Russ, and I sat there silent, used our knives as pushers, and didn't put our elbows on the table.

Later we gathered around the piano in the living room and sang carols, even Russell, who had been pretending he was too old for anything we all did as a family. Grandma, who was playing the piano, actually smiled at us and seemed to mean it.

"Have some more eggnog, Lacey," Grandma told me right before we went to bed. She was wearing this full-length flannel nightgown with little flowers all over it. I was in a giant T-shirt, a black one with a grinning skull on it. Not very Christmasy, but all the rest of my big Tees were in the laundry.

"All right," I said, even though I had already brushed my teeth and I hated the way milk made my mouth taste after I had drunk it. Everytime Grandma said anything all evening, I had said, "All right."

She gave me a glass of eggnog. I drank it. We climbed into bed. "Good night, doll," Grandma said before she rolled over.

In my nightmare, I turned into a doll. I had a string you could pull to make me talk. Grandma pulled the string, and I said, "Hello. My name is Talky Lacey. Will you be my friend?" She cut the pull ring off the end of the string so no one could pull it anymore. Then she dressed me in a really fancy dress and put me on a high shelf.

I woke up lying on the living room floor. I couldn't move.

I lay there blinking at the ceiling, watching the twinkles cast by the white lights on the white tree, and tried to figure out why my arms and legs were locked into position.

Well, of course, I was a doll.

No, I wasn't.

Sure I was. A doll with no talk string. All I had to do was sit around and look pretty.

Tears leaked out of my eyes, and then I rolled my head and saw Brian. He was sitting hunched over, knees up, hands flat on the floor, tongue-tip sticking out of his mouth. He had on red pajamas with the rockets all over them. His hair stuck up in spikes. He stared straight ahead.

"What are you?" I whispered.

"A stuffed dog." His words were smooshed because he said them with his tongue sticking out.

"Where's Russ?"

"Over there."

I turned my head and saw Russ, who was wearing brown flannel pajamas. He leaned against the wall, his feet far apart, his arms outspread. "Russ," I whispered. "What are you supposed to be?"

"A gingerbread man," he whispered.

I could roll my head. I tried to sit up, but nothing besides my neck and eyes worked.

Okay, this was another nightmare, right? I'd only dreamed that I woke up the first time. I tried to pinch myself awake, but I couldn't move my hand.

"Grandma put a spell on us," Russ whispered.

"Naw. It's only a nightmare."

"Woof," said Brian.

We lay, sat, and stood there the rest of the night. I watched dawn lighten the curtains and waited to wake up, but I didn't.

Hours went by. Eventually I smelled coffee, and heard Mom and Dad in the kitchen. Dad said, "I wonder what's keeping the kids? Usually they'd be up way before now trying to find out what's in the presents."

"The kids," said Grandma's voice. "I forgot." She came into the living room a minute later with a tray of eggnog cups. She knelt beside me. "Sit up, now, Lacey, and have some eggnog. What? You've been crying? But you've been such a good girl."

As soon as she told me to sit up, I sat up. She handed me the cup and I drank, even though by now I'd figured out that she had drugged the eggnog. I couldn't stop myself.

"Here, Brian. Have a drink. Good boy." She patted Brian on the head. "Here, Russell. Drink up. That's it. Now, you're all going to be on your best behavior, aren't you? No shouting, no breaking anything, no swearing. Well, hell. No talking, how about that? You just do what I tell you, and everything will be fine. Oh, you can say thank you when you ought to. Hurry along and get dressed now."

She made us drink another cup of eggnog before we left that afternoon. "This has been our best Christmas ever, kids. And we'll do it all again next year just the same, won't we? Yes, we will. Have seconds. You can be such good children when you're treated right." She gave us each a kiss on the forehead. Mom and Dad beamed in the background.

On the way home, I sat in the middle of the back seat with my feet on the hump and hugged the new doll Grandma had given me for Christmas and cried without making a sound. Brian didn't jab me with his elbow even once. Grandma had given him a stuffed dog. He tossed it into the back of the station wagon and threw his coat over it. Russ had a plate of gingerbread boys on his lap, but he never opened the ClingWrap.

"What a beautiful day," Mom said. "You kids sure liked Grandma's eggnog, didn't you? She gave me her secret recipe. Maybe I'll make some when we get home."

Dad said, "I don't know. I think we've had enough. We should save it for special occasions."

"Well," said Mom, "tonight is still Christmas, and the Lewises are coming over."

The Lewises. Our horrible cousins, Dad's sister's kids. They were the reason I never had any toys that worked the day after Christmas.

I glanced at Brian, and he looked back.

I didn't know what to wish for.   Ω

Nina Kiriki Hoffman is the author of scads of stories and books, including A Stir of Bones *(2003). She is also a dynamite musician, as anybody who attended a certain session at the 2004 World Fantasy Convention knows.*

SIX TAILORS

Dying female, three bells short of heaven,
The witch within her spirit wakes at last
To know herself unknown — yet unforgiven,
Dying female. Three bells short of heaven,
She spurns the cassok crows & slips unshriven
Into a sweeter future from this past
Dying. Female, three bells short of heaven,
The witch within her spirit wakes at last.

— Ann K. Schwader

SET

by Charles L. Harness

illustrated by Keith Minnion

[Ed. Note: *Dr. Tahia Halim was a famous Egyptologist as well as (in her day) an ardent Fascist and admirer of Benito Mussolini. As stipulated in her will, these papers are opened to the public fifty years after her death in 1955. They may throw some light on why an autopsy found no heart in the corpse of Il Duce.*

[*There are three separate papers (I, II, and III), evidently written at different times, all in the handwriting of Dr. Halim. We offer editorial commentary as may be appropriate.*]

I

Events following the death of Benito Mussolini are well-documented. First, he was strung upside down on the fence in Piazzale Loreto in a petrol station near the railway station.

[Ed. Note: *Today the petrol shed has been replaced by a MacDonald's restaurant.*] After its day in the petrol station the body was taken to the hospital (the Instituto di Medicina Legale) of the University of Milan. There the American military autopsied it. They removed some brain tissue and sent the fragments to St. Elizabeth's Hospital in Washington D.C. for examination for syphilis. They found none. They were also asked whether they had received his heart, which seemed to be missing. This they denied, and indeed there is nothing in the transmitting papers about a heart. [Ed. Note: *On 25 March 1966 the remnants of brain matter were returned to his wife Rachele in six test tubes in a wooden box by the United States ambassador in Rome, marked "Mussolini."*]

The autopsy done, his body was hurriedly and anonymously buried in the Musocco cemetery outside Milan. At midnight 22 April 1946 the tomb was robbed by a trio of Fascist fanatics. The body was eventually recovered in the Certosa of Pavia — the charterhouse of a Carthusian monastery. He was re-buried, this time in the Capuchin chapel at Cerro Maggiore. It was then noted that the heart was missing.

A review of the chaotic history and route of the corpse turned up no trace of the missing organ.

[Ed. Note: *In 1957 the corpse was moved to its final resting place, the family mausoleum in the cemetery of San Cassiano at Predappio. Today, heart or no heart, it is a great tourist attraction.*]

So — what happened to his heart?

[Ed. Note: *We go back to Dr. Halim's notes. Two documents have surfaced that throw light on the question. First is II, Dr. Halim's memorandum of a meeting in 1922 with Mussolini and the Fascist Quadrumvir.*]

II

Il Duce opened the meeting. There were five men, all wearing their famous black shirts, and a woman, wearing black. "We're all here. Let me make the introductions. I present Dr.Tahia Halim, our agent in Cairo."

I stood, smiled at the group, and bowed. They saw a middle-aged woman, dressed in simple but elegant gray.

He continued. "Doctor, we have here the four members of our Quadrumvir: Italo Balbo, war hero, famous for burning communist buildings." Balbo bowed. "And General Emilio De Bono, our Chief of Police." A tall slim man with a pointed white beard stood and bowed solemnly. "Cesare De Vecchi. The general and De Vecchi are personal friends of Margherita, the queen mother — who greatly admires us. And number four, Michele Bianchi, our National Party Secretary." (Bows.) "These are the men who have organized our March on Rome." He turned toward the woman. "And finally, our valued consigliera, Margherita Sarfatti, editor of our journal, Gerarchia." Here he paused, turned dark eyes on me, then back to the men. "Dr. Halim is an expert on the archeology of ancient Egypt. She has written articles, books praised by Breasted, Petrie and others in her field. Tonight she brings us interesting news, plus certain artifacts, and a proposal that may help our March on Rome. Doctor?"

"Thank you, *Duce*. The story is this. An Englishman, Howard Carter, is presently involved in a dig in southern Egypt, in the Valley of the Kings. He has in fact made a fantastic discovery. The news will be out next week. He has discovered the thirty-three-hundred-year-old tomb of a pharaoh, we think named Tut-Ankh-Amen, mostly intact, with the mummy still untouched."

"Extraordinary," whispered Margherita Sarfatti. She and the five men leaned across the table toward me.

I continued.

"In the entrance way they found a guardian statue, the god Anubis, with raised spear. The spear pointed down at a figure in black obsidian, a statuette with the face of a pig. This was Set, the god of darkness, a very powerful god. Whoever possesses this god, shares his power."

They waited in strained silence as I gathered breath. "The tomb will be opened officially in a few weeks. I estimate toward the end of November. There is already much excitement and confusion. The diggers left late that first night, but left the tomb and tunnel well lit and a couple of soldiers as guards. But we planned well. The lights suddenly failed. There was confusion, the guards stumbled around in the dark. That's when we took the statue of the god."

Sarfatti looked startled. "You *robbed* the tomb?"

I smiled, shrugged delicately.

"So where is the statue?" asked General De Bono.

"Right here." I walked over to a corner of the room and pulled a tarpaulin from a black diorite statue about 70 centimeters high, with the unsmiling face of a pig. Certain other things lay by the statue.

"The point?" demanded Balbo.

I said, "He can help our March on Rome."

"O Roma o morte," murmured *Il Duce.* ["Rome, or death."]

"I don't get it," said Bianchi. "How can a stupid stone help our March? Do we carry him along on a float, and he showers magic right and left. What —"

"None of that, " I said. "Sr. Bianchi, look at how the matter stands at this very moment. In the city, General Pugliese commands twelve thousand troops, with armored cars and artillery. They cover Santa Marinella, Monterotondo, and Tivoli, the three points of entry for our marchers. We know Prime Minister Facta has laid on the king's desk an edict proclaiming martial law, and we know the king has promised to sign it. When that happens Pugliese's troops will surely fire on our marchers. The March will collapse. We — everyone one of us — will be hunted down, arrested, imprisoned, some of us will be shot."

"So?" said De Vecchi.

"So listen to her," said *Il Duce.*

I continued. "We will petition the god Set to work on the mind of Victor Emmanuel. A precise ceremony is involved. It is absolutely necessary to go through with it if we are to succeed. When it is completed, *Duce,* you must ask the great god to make the king fearful, make him doubt the loyalty of his officers, make him foresee bloodshed, chaos, even civil war if he signs that edict. He will doubt and dither and finally he cannot bring himself to sign the order to fire. We march. Facta resigns. You *Duce,* enter history. The king appoints you prime minister and asks you to form a cabinet. You win everything."

"Ah . . . everything?" he whispered. He looked around at the group.

"Yes, *Duce,* everything," I said, "but first the ceremony."

"The ceremony . . ."

"Yes. We must awaken the god."

"This ceremony," said Sarfatti, "painless, I trust?"

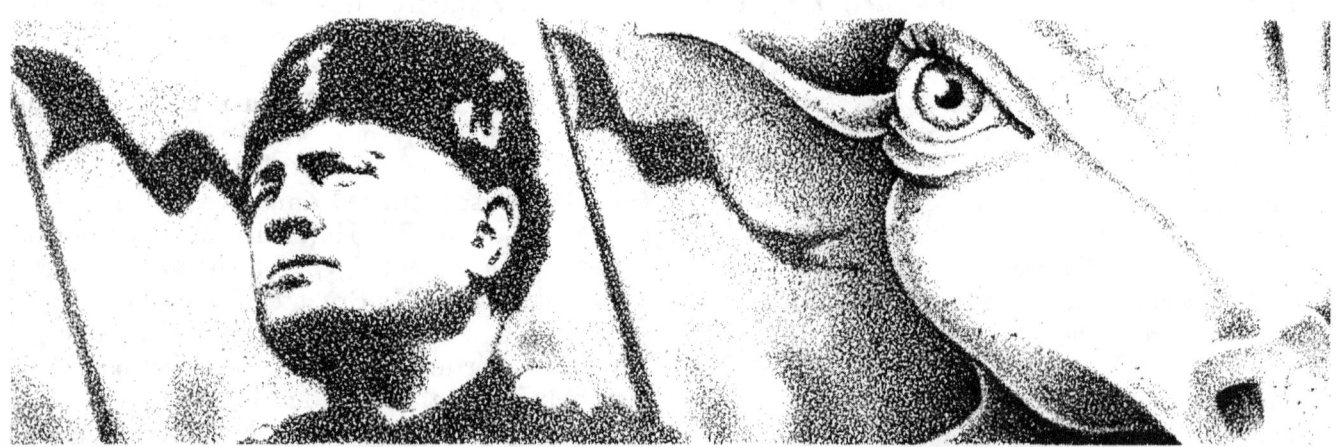

"Absolutely. It is called, 'Opening the Mouth of the God.' It awakens his five senses — vision, hearing, smell, touch, taste. On awakening he may answer our petition, but he will also surely take vengeance on those who opened the tomb. Lord Carnarvon financed the dig and will die. Howard Carter did the actual work but he has undertaken a ritual cleansing, with suitable apologies to the pharaoh. He may survive. But we must hurry. The king could sign that edict at any moment. The procedure is not difficult, and all is ready at hand. I have everything you will need."

"Va bene. Let us start."

I handed him a brush and a cup of milk and spoke my instructions in a low monotone.

"First, daub the lips of the god with milk."

He did.

"Next, embrace the god three times."

He did.

"Now touch his mouth with this haunch of a slaughtered bull."

He lifted the carcass fragment as ordered. "Now touch the mouth with this sacred adze." He did. "And now with your right index finger, with this white paint trace your full name on the front face of the statue block."

He did — *Benito Amilcare Andrea Mussolini.*

"Now face the god and say this to him." I handed him a short typewritten script.

He recited in a confident sonorous voice:

"Thy mouth was closed, but I have set in order for thee thy mouth and thy teeth. I open for thee thy mouth, I open for thee thy two eyes. I have opened thy mouth with the instrument of Anubis, with the iron implement with which the mouths of the gods were opened in the Beginning, when Ptah formed the Earth. Horus, open the mouth! Horus, open the mouth! Horus hath opened the mouth of the dead, as he in times of old opened the mouth of Osiris with the iron, which came forth from thee, O mighty Set, with the iron instrument with which he opened the mouths of the gods. He hath opened thy mouth with it. Thou shalt walk and speak, and thy body shall be with the great company of all the gods." Now the *Duce*-Priest raised the adze and touched it to Set's mouth, completing the spell that would give the dark god breath.

He had barely completed the last words when a darkness suddenly fell over the room. Mussolini dropped the adze. I knew he was trembling. But he immediately got hold of himself, took a couple of deep breaths. "Doctor?"

"Yes." I handed him a flashlight. "Quickly now, ask for the success of the March! It's on the script. Read!"

He did not hesitate.

"O thou great god of darkness, hear my plea! In the name of a greater Italy, I beg you, honor our March on Rome!"

I had anticipated what would happen, but it still left me half paralyzed. Did *Il Duce's* plea have any effect at all? No way to tell. We all looked down where the god should be. Something was there. *Il Duce* stepped back nervously. The lights came on again. Mussolini blinked.

I held up a hand. "He is awake," I hissed.

We waited.

The phone rang. Mussolini jumped, startled. Then he nodded toward Margherita and she picked it up. "Pronto." They all listened. After a moment she grinned and turned to Mussolini. "It's the Quirinal, Salandro, the king's secretary. Call off the March and he'll give the Fascists four seats in parliament."

Il Duce snorted. "For six hundred thousand marchers, four seats? No. Hang up."

She did.

We waited.

The phone rang again. Sarfatti answered. Her eyebrows raised. "Yes, majesty. Just a moment." She handed the phone to Mussolini. He held it out, we could all hear.

"Signore," the king said stiffly, "we did not sign the edict. Facta has resigned. We invite you to become prime minister, form a cabinet. Do you accept?"

On that night of October 31, 1922 Benito Mussolini presented his roster of ministers to the king and at 39 became the youngest Italian prime minister in history. Later that same night (or very early morning) he relaxed with his friends in his suite at the Savoia. I was included.

Carlo Balbo said to him, *"Duce,* you are finally complete master of the situation."

Mussolini was thoughtful. "Yes, I have opportunities never before enjoyed by an Italian prime minister. I look beyond Italy to Africa. You know, Carlo, our empire once ruled much of Africa, from Egypt to Morocco. Now it's only Libya and a piece of East Africa. We once had it all. We'll have it again."

"England?" said General De Bono. "League of Nations?"

"Italy, not Britain, must rule the Mediterranean. And the League is a joke. Sanctions on arms? Under Sanctions, Ethiopia can receive no arms, but Italy can manufacture all it wants. The outcome cannot be in doubt."

The phone rang. Balbo took it, listened for a moment. "It's for you, doctor."

I took it, listened for several minutes. "It's our man in Cairo. An hour ago a cobra got into the cage and swallowed Howard Carter's pet canary. Set has begun the curse."

"A coincidence," muttered Balbo.

"Maybe not," said Sarfatti.

"There's an interesting rumor," I said. "Madame Velma, a well-known Cairo psychic, says it's the hand of Set. She has warned Lord Carnarvon, if he returns to the tomb, he will die."

[**Ed. Note:** *They did not have long to wait. Carnarvon died at 2 a.m. April 5, 1923 of an infection on his cheek. At the precise moment of his death all the lights in Cairo went out; his three-legged terrier howled and dropped dead. And several others associated with the tomb died soon thereafter: Carnarvon's younger brother; an x-ray specialist en route to examine the mummy; plus several others — famous people, with several murders and suicides.*]

III

[**Ed. Note:** *We come forward in time with a brief summary. It is 1940. World War II has begun. France falls. Mussolini joins Hitler. After Dunkirk Hitler turns on Russia. Pearl Harbor brings the United States into the war and soon Germany is fighting on two fronts — the East and Italy.*

[*Italy is losing. On July 25, 1943 Victor Emmanuel dismissed Mussolini as prime minister. Italy surrendered to the Allies September 8, 1943 and switched sides. Italy was obliged to fight her old ally, Germany. Hitler immediately ordered the German army to occupy what was left of Italy. D-Day came, and now Germany was fighting on three fronts: East, West, and Italy. Mussolini tried to escape to Switzerland in a German convoy. On April 27, 1945 he was recognized by partisans, seized and shot to death.*]

Given the facts of the case I believe this is what happened next:

There was at first a darkness. Then everything gradually became luminous and Mussolini saw that he was standing in a great chamber. He looked about in astonishment and fear. In front of him on a raised bench a radiant red-robed figure sat. To the right of the figure stood a man with the head of an ibis. He held a writing desk.

To the left, next to a door, sat a jackal-headed man.

The central figure spoke in a clear even voice. "I am Osiris. Benito Amilcare Andrea Mussolini, you were shot to death at 1610 hours on the 28th of April 1945 on the Via XXIV Maggio in the hamlet of San Guilino di Mezzegra. You now stand before your Court of Judgment." He pointed to the creature with the jackal head. "Anubis guards the door into the next world. Thoth —" He nodded toward the ibis-headed man. "— will write it all down." He motioned to the shadowy figures behind him. "The Shenit will weigh you in the balance."

Mussolini's mouth dropped. He looked at the judge, at the others. "Osiris . . . ? Balance . . . ?" He noted then, on the dais, to the side of Osiris, a balance. In one pan was a feather, in the other a beating heart. He clutched at his chest. His felt nothing. His heart was gone. *That* was his heart . . . being measured against a *feather?* So far, the scale seemed to be in perfect balance. He scowled. "What pagan nonsense is this? I am a Catholic. If I am dead I go to heaven. It's already decided."

"*Signore,*" said Osiris mildly, "when you joined us, you renounced Christ."

"No! Osiris, your honor, that's not the way it was. Ask Set, he can tell you."

"Ah, you know the dark god, he who murdered me, cut me up into fourteen pieces?"

Mussolini blinked, bowed his head. "Majesty, I did not know about that." He looked up. "But, your honor, here you are recovered."

A brief silence.

Then Osiris asked, "How did you meet Set?"

"Well, your honor, I rescued him from the tomb of Tut-Ankh-Amen. He was locked in eternal sleep. I opened his mouth. I returned him to life. He is my friend. If I must be judged here, please let him speak for me."

Osiris frowned. "Is this true? Let us examine the record. Thoth, what happened?" Thoth conferred briefly with the great judge. Osiris nodded, looked down across the bench.

Someone tapped Mussolini on the shoulder. He turned to face a tall, mightily built creature — in human form except for the red-bristled head of a pig. He wore a red cape, draped loosely around his shoulders. Mussolini stared. *"Set?"*

Set laughed. "Yes. And here to help you once again." He bowed to the jackal-headed figure. "Ah, Anubis, lord of the land of the dead. Will you open the door for my client? We shall see." He looked up. "I remind you, Osiris, my brother, without my cleansing powers, life would soon degenerate into fruity glut. I am the corrector of flabby excesses, I cut away dead flesh, dead ideas, dead customs. I am necessary for the proper flow of life. In that capacity I am here to speak for Benito Mussolini."

"We accept you," said Osiris. He nodded to Thoth. "Take it all down."

Set turned to his client. "Offer your confession. Talk to your heart. I will put the words in your mouth."

The accused bowed humbly. He addressed his heart, beating quietly in the balance. "I have never personally killed a man . . . but for the good of the Fascist state I have ordered many men killed."

"Innocent men," said Set. "We speak only the truth here."

"Communists," said Mussolini. "A danger to the state."

"Continue," said Osiris.

"I have taken many mistresses, but I have always remained faithful to Rachele. I have never taken another's property, except in the service of the state. I have never lied or betrayed anyone, except in the service of the state. I have never burnt a building or broken a treaty except in the service of the state. I am pure . . . I am pure . . . I am pure."

"Address the forty-two," said Set. "Here are the words."

"Ah, of course . . . the gods of the forty-two nomes of Egypt." Osiris recited the forty-two names in a sing-song.

"Now the canopic gods," prodded Set. "No . . . wait. . . skip that. Your internals were never properly stored in the four canopic jars."

Osiris said, "You ordered the death of your political adversary, Giacomo Matteotti."

Mussolini nodded. "He voted against me."

"You concurred in the execution of Count Ciano, your son-in-law."

Mussolini sighed. "It was necessary. He wanted to depose me."

"You caused the deaths of over a million men, women, children."

Mussolini shuddered. "Surely not so many?"

The great judge spoke in a grim monotone. "Four hundred thousand Italian soldiers in World War Two, to that add your soldiers killed in Libya, Ethiopia, the Spanish Civil War. To that add the helpless men, women, children your soldiers killed. Over a million, *Signore.*"

Mussolini bowed his head. "Perhaps . . . yes. But always for the state. They were mostly communists."

There was a pause.

Thoth signaled. "The record is finished."

"Now," said Osiris, "the Shenit weighs the feather against your heart. The feather is Maat, daughter of Ra — righteousness, truth, law. If Anubis is to open the door to the beautiful afterworld for you, Benito, your heart must be True of Voice. It must exactly balance the Feather. But if the heart is heavy with evil, you will be eternally damned. You will be thrown into the burning lakes, where flaming water is your only drink, and you are delivered to cruel demons, tormentors of the damned, who dwell amid walls of living snakes, on floors of boiling water, and under roofs of fire." He paused and turned to his right. "So then, how says the balance?"

"Look!" whispered Set. He pointed. The balance was shuddering. "The Shenit can't make up their minds!"

And now the arm began to sway. First the heart was up, then the feather. Then slowly the heart sank.

"I am damned," groaned Mussolini. "Va bene." He sighed heavily. "Perhaps it is just. At least all accounts are now squared. I owe nothing to anyone."

Osiris spoke. "Benito Mussolini, we have listened to you, and to the million people you have killed. We find you guilty, and we must sentence you to eternal damnation. However, my brother Set urges mercy. For his sake we commute your sentence. You will neither pass through the door of Anubis nor into the burning lakes. You will simply pass out of existence and into oblivion, as though you had never been born. *Anemut, come!*"

A creature with the head of a hippopotamus and the body of a crocodile emerged from the side of the chamber, waddled toward the scale, snapped up the heart in one gulp, and vanished.

And so did Benito Amilcare Andrea Mussolini.

Ω

Charles Harness is the author of such classic SF novels as The Paradox Men. *Much of his work has been reprinted by NESFA Press. We are very sorry to learn that he passed away recently.*

RIPPER!

by William F. Nolan

illustrated by George Barr

Second of Two Parts

What Has Gone Before:

On a foggy English night in November of 1888, near London Bridge, two police constables arrive in time to rescue a woman from getting her throat cut. They pursue the attacker onto the Bridge and, in the struggle that ensues, the figure is struck by a police club and falls into the Thames, dislodging a stone on the Bridge railing that follows the body into the river. The two constables wonder: could it have been Jack the Ripper?

August of 2004, Lake Havasu City, Arizona: The original London Bridge has been shipped from England and reconstructed, stone by stone, above a branch of the Colorado River. A simulated English village has been constructed around the Bridge and the area is now one of Arizona's top tourist attractions.

After a long, cross-country drive, Dave and Lia Kelley, en route to Los Angeles, arrive in the area late in the evening. In the pub, over dinner, they learn that a final stone was recently discovered at the bottom of the Thames River, after resting there for more than a hundred years. The stone has been shipped to Lake Havasu and will be officially fitted into the Bridge the following morning. Lia wants to see it, but Dave is bushed and retires to their motel, leaving her to walk over London Bridge alone. She accidentally cuts her hand on the railing, and her blood drips onto the newly-placed stone. A dark mist rises from the blood and a cloaked figure is reborn.

Ripper!

The next day Angie Shepherd, who runs a boat service, discovers Lia's body floating in the river, her throat cut. Police detective Steve Gregory, an ex-cop from Chiacgo new to the Havasu force, is put in charge of the investigation, assisted by his partner Joe Nez. When the Bridge area is closed to the public for an evidence search, Steve comes into conflict with Anson Whitfield, the city mayor, who wants the village open for tourists and dismisses the murder as a random act of violence by a passing transient. Gregory rejects this theory,

by William F. Nolan

but as yet has no theory of his own to replace it. Police Chief Pete Dawson also feels that the killer is a transient, putting Gregory in conflict with his immediate superior.

Elaine Phillips, a journalist from San Francisco, becomes the Ripper's next victim. Her disappearance rouses Gregory's suspicions, but he is still unsure of just what is happening.

But there is a peculiar stranger in town who speaks with a British accent. Could *he* be the murderer?

When lab tests reveal that the killer wore period clothing from the 19th century, and used a weapon flecked with equally old blood, Gregory begins research into the crimes of Jack the Ripper as a new idea begins to form in his mind.

The Story Continues . . .

The Vicar's Dirk Night Club:

The dance floor was laced by flashing pinwheels of multi-colored lights, and the local band onstage — Havasu's English — was rocking.

"You're a good dancer," Angie said.

"Well, I can dance better than I can fish," he answered, spinning her out for a turn.

"Want to sit down?" she asked.

"Now who's out of shape?"

They moved to a distant table on the patio where the background music became a softened counterpoint to their conversation.

"Thank you," said Gregory.

"For what?"

"For letting me talk. I feel better, now."

"I'm glad," she said. She instinctively pressed her hand over his as they both realized that a bond had formed between them.

"I've been meaning to ask you: What made you become a cop?"

"My old man was a cop," Steve said. "So was *his* old man. Guess it just runs in the family."

"Didn't you ever want to be anything else . . . when you were little?"

"Oh, sure, but I finally realized that I just didn't have what it takes."

"To be what?"

"A prima ballerina."

They were laughing as the waitress arrived with wine spritzers.

Gregory raised his glass. "Here's to people who understand."

They clinked glasses and sipped their wine.

"I want to understand you," Angie said. "I think you're very much worth understanding."

"What about you?" he asked. "What did you want to be when you were a little girl?"

"Straight answer?"

"Straight."

"Well, I never got to college," Angie said. "Dad had this boat service, and when he retired, I ended up doing what he did."

"With a marriage in between."

"Yeah. Larry and I had known each other since we were little kids; we were high school sweethearts. When I was growing up, I *really* wanted to be a psychologist — I wanted to help others with their emotional problems. So many lives get screwed up, and I wanted to help."

Gregory touched her cheek. "And that's just what you wound up doing. Helping *me*. I sure have been screwed up since things went bad back in Chicago." He looked intently into her eyes. "I'm glad I found you, Angie. You're becoming very important to me."

"You *mean* that, don't you?"

"Yes."

He leaned forward, and their lips met with warm, gathering hunger.

Bank of the Colorado River. Morning:

The group of boisterous fourth and fifth graders, happy to be out of the classroom on a field trip, were sitting around Mr. Hought — the new teacher in town — whose still-boyish demeanor had made him the instant favorite of the elementary school set.

". . . and that's one of the reasons why we're all lucky to live in Havasu: we have so many different kinds of birds that visit us each year," he said. Hought nodded to a bright-eyed ten-year-old. "Judy, can you tell me a kind of river duck that we sometimes see here in Havasu?"

"Mallard," she replied.

He beamed a delighted-teacher smile at her. "Correct! The mallard. And do you know how to identify the *male* mallard?"

"His neck is green."

"You're right! Now, we all know that a female mallard has a light brown head, with dark streaks along —"

Judy abruptly interrupted him, pointing toward the river current. "Look, Mr. Hought . . . a *floating lady."*

The children surged forward as Mr. Hought gasped in shock at the gruesome sight of a woman's corpse bumping the shoreline.

Her throat had been cut.

Elaine Phillips.

Lake Havasu Library.
September 8, 2004. Night:

Lynn Chandler yawned and stretched. The wall clock said 7:48. Twelve minutes to closing time. Except for the periodic chirp of the library's resident cricket, it was quiet as Boot Hill cemetery — and with every other overhead light out as an electricity conservation measure, the main room was deeply shadowed. The tall stacks loomed in the background, phantom-shapes in the deepening Southwestern night.

Lynn pushed aside a pile of books and eased back in her desk chair. She was tired, and looking forward to a hot shower and a full night's sleep. A tuna sandwich and green salad take out from Blimpie's, then home to feed Tabby and Crinkles (her cat companions of several years), and she could still be in bed before ten.

Tomorrow she would be up before dawn, for a six mile walk along the river, which would end just as the sun came up over the eastern horizon. Then her great-grandmother's traditional Papago breakfast: eggs scrambled with tepary beans, fresh spinach, and onions. She'd add a slice of cantaloupe, a mug of white sage tea, and her many nutritional supplements. From her own family history Lynn knew the scientific fact that fifty percent of Papago and Pima Indians develop full-blown diabetes by the time they're adults. Half-Papago, she was meticulous about both her nutrition and her exercise program so she could avoid what so many medical authorities seemed to think was inevitable.

Her solo daily routine seldom varied, and this was beginning to depress her. By rights, she should be out on the town past midnight with a muscled hunk, instead of being tucked away in her bed before ten. Going with Angie to the occasional Friday night dinner, followed by a film at the multi-plex, just didn't cut it.

Ah, she thought — maybe I'll get lucky.

A faint sound between cricket chirps. Angie raised her head. The sound came from the far end of the stacks. Near the back door. Had she locked it? Yes, she was certain she had; she could remember locking it after the late afternoon FedEx delivery. Now the library was silent again. Maybe she had imagined the sound.

She picked up her purse and was in the act of switching off the reading lamp on her desk when she heard the strange sound again. Louder this time. Distinct.

Someone was in the library.

Lynn pivoted in horror as a dark, swift-gliding figure rushed toward her. Before she could scream, a blade was buried in her throat.

Lynn would never scream again.

Lake Havasu City Police Department.
Office of the Chief of Police.
Morning:

Startled by the knock on his closed door, Pete Dawson looked up in irritation from the columns of figures on his budget proposal. "In!" he growled.

Steve Gregory entered, walked over to the desk, and put down a folder. "Figured you'd want to see these."

Dawson opened the folder and removed several 8x10 glossy photographs. On top: a boot print in soft earth; underneath: a picture of a women's scarf in an intricately interwoven, geometric Hopi design.

The chief looked up at Gregory. "What about 'em?"

"The boot print is from the river bank, a spot close to the village. Where we think the killer dumped Elaine Phillips."

"How do you figure?"

"The scarf is hers. She bought it at Windsor Garden Fashions in the village. Antique, one of a kind — from Hotevilla. Paid almost five hundred dollars for it, but said she'd be wearing it for the rest of her life. Planned to make it a signature piece for photos on all the books she expected to write. When she was put into the water, the scarf snagged on the branch of a cottonwood tree."

Dawson grunted. "And since her throat was cut — just like the Kelley woman — there's a good chance it's the same perp."

"Same MO. And the lab report indicates that the murder weapon is probably identical." Gregory

hesitated. "I want permission to close down the village. Both murders are directly tied to that area."

Dawson stood up, walked to the window, and stared out. "If I shut down the village again, I'll catch hell from Whitfield and the City Council."

"And if you *don't* shut it down, more people could die at the hands of this maniac." Gregory's voice was intense. "He's *out* there, Pete. He's already killed two women, and I think he's going to kill more."

Dawson swung back to his desk. "Once the village is closed, we may as well close the entire city. Tourism is what keeps Havasu alive — or hadn't you noticed?"

"I know you'll get a lot of heat from Whitfield and his gang, but we can't risk any more lives."

Dawson sat down at his desk and looked at the photos again. He stared at Gregory. "Do *you* believe this creep is going to quit killing just because we close the village?"

"We won't know until we try," said Gregory. "But at least no more women will get their throats cut on London Bridge."

Dawson tapped his desk with tense fingers. "How long do you want the village closed?"

"As long as it takes to catch the killer."

The chief scowled and shook his head. "No good, Steve. We don't know when, or even *if*, he'll be found. The best I can do is post plainclothes police officers in the village — but I can't authorize a shutdown."

Gregory clenched his fists. "You mean *won't*, not can't."

"I'm responsible to the public. I have sworn duties to this community that go beyond strict police work."

"Sure . . . sure you do."

Steve Gregory's face was tight with anger as he walked out of Dawson's office.

Gregory's Apartment.
That night:

The grilled cheese sandwich he was fixing for dinner had just finished browning when the ringing phone broke into his reverie. "Gregory here," he said.

"It's Angie. I'm worried."

"What about?"

"Lynn. She didn't show up today at the library, and she *never* misses work. When I tried to call her, I couldn't get an answer. I have a key to her

place so I drove over, but she wasn't there. And she hadn't been there for awhile."

"How do you know?"

"Her cats were ravenous with hunger. Lynn would *never* leave Tabby and Crinkles unfed — and she'd never go away without first telling me to take care of them, either."

Steve could hear the fear in Angie's voice. "Whew," he said.

"I think something awful has happened to her," said Angie.

Gregory cleared his throat. "Can I come over now? I'll take a formal statement from you about Lynn, and that will start the ball rolling on a missing person investigation." He paused for a moment. "I was going to call you anyway, because I'm working on a new theory, and I'd like to talk it over with you."

"I'll be here," she said.

Saguaro View Apartments.
Night:

Edward Latting carried a newspaper down the corridor to number thirteen. He entered, sat down on the bed, unfolded the paper, and scanned the headlined story:

SECOND MURDER SHOCKS
HAVASU CITY
Body Discovered In River
Near London Bridge

Latting's eyes narrowed. He tossed the paper aside, walked to the closet, and removed his black leather carryall. He ran his fingers slowly and carefully — almost lovingly — over the contents. The bag contained plastique explosives. Satisfied, he closed the carryall and stood in front of the framed print of London Bridge. He stared at the print, taking in all its pastel details. His eyes darkened.

Removing a knife from his coat, he leaned forward, then slashed viciously at the print, cutting a jagged "X" across the glass.

Angie Shepherd's Home on the River.
Night:

Angie and Steve Gregory sat across the table from each other in the kitchen nook. Her face was clouded, and she was clearly distraught. Her movements were mechanical and robot-like. She had given him all the relevant information about Lynn that she had — and he'd dutifully jotted it down in his notebook — but she realized that, in truth, she had very little of value to tell him.

"When I leave here," Steve said, "I'll go straight to the department and file a formal missing person's report, then I'll authorize a statewide APB. If she's out there, there's a good chance we can find her."

"If she was alive, she would've contacted me," Angie said, very softly.

He put his hand over hers. "Don't go there, Angie. We don't know what happened. You can't make any assumptions right now."

"Well, I'm going over to Lynn's place and bring Tabby and Crinkles back here." Her eyes filled with tears. "I think they need a new home, and that's what Lynn would have wanted me to do."

"We'll do everything we can to find her," he said.

An awkward silence between them.

Then: "I've been working on a new theory," he said. "I think it's important."

Angie visibly straightened her posture and took in a slow, deep breath. "Okay, tell me about it."

"We found a tiny fragment of cloth under one of Lia Kelley's fingernails. The lab determined that it was over a century old. I think the killer bought the coat from an antique shop — to match his assumed identity."

"What identity?"

"I'll get to that." He leaned toward her. "Next, take the *way* he killed his victims — by cutting their throats. My supposition is that he did it with a scalpel. Probably an antique; old, like the clothes. A surgeon's scalpel."

Angie winced. "Steve, I don't think I'm up to this."

"It's important for you to know everything," he said.

She sighed. "Okay. Go on."

"Consider the vital dates: August 7th, when Lia Kelley was murdered on London Bridge — and August 31st, the last night Elaine Phillips, the reporter, was seen alive."

"What's the connection?" she asked.

"Just wait," he answered. "Let's add a *third* date: September 8th."

"When Lynn disappeared," she said dully.

He put his hand over hers again. "It *may* be the night when Lynn became a victim of the same killer."

Angie shuddered, and tears formed in her eyes.

"But there's no *proof*. I mean, they haven't found her body . . ."

"The body of Elaine Phillips wasn't found until it washed ashore."

"Then you believe —"

"I believe that *someone* was murdered on September 8th. I just don't know who."

Angie's voice was strained. "I've been telling myself that Lynn will show up, that she's really all right somehow, but — in my heart — I know I'll never see her again."

Steve Gregory waited a long moment for Angie to absorb the shock, then continued: "The three dates I've named match exactly the dates of a trio of murders attributed to Jack the Ripper, in London's Whitechapel district, more than a century ago. Between August 7th and November 9th, 1888, six women were slaughtered in that area. The killer vanished the same year. I've been doing a lot of research and I found this."

He handed her a Xerox copy of a newspaper article.

"Read the headline," said Gregory.

"Dying Constable Reveals Possible Solution to Ripper Mystery."

Gregory leaned toward Angie. "Constable Jonathan Graham made a death bed statement in which he claimed to have killed Jack the Ripper at London Bridge on the night of November 15, 1888. He said he couldn't *prove* that the man who fell into the Thames that night was the Ripper, which is why he'd kept silent about it. But there were no more Ripper murders after that date."

Angie sighed. "You believe that the man who died that night was Jack the Ripper?"

"I do."

"But what has this got to do with —"

"Our killer wears clothing from the same period. He probably uses a doctor's scalpel, very possibly an antique scalpel also from that era. He cuts his victim's throats. And he strikes in the vicinity of London Bridge."

Angie wasn't making the connection.

"In his deranged mental state," Steve continued, "our guy identifies himself with this iconic killer from the past. This gives him a sense of

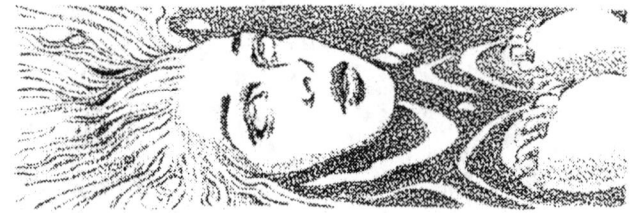

invincibility. I believe we're dealing with a nut-case who actually *thinks* he's Jack the Ripper."

"That's a pretty wild theory," she said.

"It's the only one that fits."

"What will Pete Dawson say when you tell him?"

"I already have. He thinks that ex-Chicago police detectives have bizarre imaginations."

"Meaning he doesn't buy it?"

"No. Not yet. But he *will*."

"Why?"

"Because if the pattern continues, two more murders will occur on the night of September 30th . . . and then he'll be *forced* to believe me." Steve ground his hands together. "But I don't intend to let two more women die just to prove I'm right. We've got to stop this guy before those murders happen."

"How?"

He looked at her. "That's a very good question."

Lake Havasu City Hall.
Parking Lot.
Early morning:

In the late 1960s, Anson Whitfield — grandson of Arizona pioneers, a University of Arizona law school graduate, and newly admitted to the Arizona bar — established his law practice in the brand new community of Lake Havasu City and began a career that eventually culminated in his election as mayor. So far as Havasu was concerned, Whitfield was "Old Money" — and he enjoyed the considerable local status that went with it. Now, when he exited his Mercedes sedan and walked toward City Hall, his attire — carefully-tailored gray suit, red bolo tie, and carved turquoise silver clasp — radiated the extreme confidence natural to small town bigwigs.

As he crossed the municipal parking lot toward City Hall, he saw a Honda drive into the other entrance. Steve Gregory jumped out of the passenger door and intercepted the mayor.

"Mayor Whitfield, we need to talk."

"Not now. I'm late for a meeting."

"This is urgent," said Gregory, blocking his path.

Whitfield scowled darkly. He hadn't approved of Gregory being hired — ex-Chicago cops with questionable backgrounds didn't belong here; it was entirely the wrong tone for tourist-oriented Havasu — and he'd had no reason to modify his opinion since, especially after he'd accidentally overheard his granddaughter refer to the new detective as "a hottie."

"What do you want?"

"We need to close down the village."

"For another useless search?"

"No, sir. For the safety of the public. The killer is still at large and we can't afford to —"

Whitfield cut him off, speaking sharply. "Did Chief Dawson order the village closed?"

"No. I'm asking you to do this voluntarily, as a gesture of public safety."

Whitfield glared at him. "Public safety is *your* job. That's what this city pays you for. And unless Chief Dawson personally orders the village shut down, it stays open."

"Your attitude stinks, Whitfield."

The older man glared with anger. "I'll tell you what stinks! Your record! You didn't fit in back east, and you don't fit in here, either. You're unstable, a misfit." He jabbed a finger into Gregory's chest. "I know all about you! I know about that thirteen-year-old kid you blew away in Chicago."

Gregory's eyes flashed. He grabbed Whitfield by his coat lapels and pushed him against the cement block wall. His fist was cocked for impact as Joe Nez rushed in to intervene. "Whoa, buddy!" He pulled his partner away. "Just ease down."

Whitfield backed toward the entrance, badly

shaken. "You're finished in this city, mister! I promise you that. Your career is *over!*"

"We'll see," said Gregory.

Whitfield entered the glass doors of City Hall as Pete Dawson quickly approached the two detectives.

"What was *that* all about?"

"I almost decked Whitfield. He was way out of line on what he said to me."

Dawson's jaw tightened. "How could you even *think* about decking the mayor?"

"I'm sorry, Pete, but the guy's an A-1 jerk."

"I'll second that," said Joe Nez.

Dawson blew out a frustrated breath. "Okay, we'll talk about this later. Right now, we have business to take care of. Cassie Nebel phoned me. Said we needed to get over there right away." He gestured toward the Honda. "You guys follow me over to the *Herald.*"

Lake Havasu City *Herald* Building. Same day:

The three men walked to the rear of the building. Inside her office, Cassie Nebel looked up from a story she was editing.

"What have you got?" asked Dawson.

Cassie handed over a sheet of paper. "Our first crackpot poem. Maybe I should frame it."

The words on the sheet were handwritten in old-fashioned script:

My dear editor:
I have composed a small poem I would like to see printed in your paper. I'm sure it will amuse your readers.

Three dead,
soon four.
The stone has told me,
there will be more.

The letter was signed: *Jack.*

Cassie was troubled. "Whitfield has been pressuring me to keep news about the killings out of the paper," she said. "I haven't decided what to do with this, but whoever this guy is, he can't count. There've been two murders, not three."

"No," Gregory corrected her. "It's three."

Cassie Nebel's eyebrows rose. "How do you figure? Lia Kelley. Elaine Phillips . . ."

". . . and Lynn Chandler," said Gregory. "The last line says it all: 'There will be more.'"

Office of the Chief of Police. Later, the same day:

Dawson perched on the side of his desk and glared at the two detectives seated on the couch. "After what you almost did to Whitfield today, this letter is the only reason I'm not kicking your rosy butt off the case, Steve. At least it proves that we *do* have a copycat Ripper working in Havasu."

". . . who just killed Lynn Chandler," added Gregory.

"Could be," said Dawson. "She's definitely missing. If she *is* dead, that would make it three."

"Think it's a good idea for Cassie to print the letter?"

Dawson shrugged. "Why not? No point in keeping it under wraps. Let's give our resident weirdo all the publicity he wants. Might help draw him into the open." He fiddled with the pen holder on his desk. "Besides, the public needs to be warned. This way, we'll have the whole county watching for him."

"What do you make of that part about 'the stone has told me there will be more'?" asked Joe.

Gregory rubbed a fist along his jaw. "I can't figure the 'stone' part, but one thing's for sure: we gotta nail this scumball, and fast." He tapped the letter on Dawson's desk. "Because if he keeps to

the Ripper's pattern, he'll kill again on September 30th."

Saguaro View Apartments. The front office. Same day:

The latest issue of the Lake Havasu City *Herald* was spread over the front desk, in front of Alma Bowers.

ANOTHER JACK THE RIPPER AT LONDON BRIDGE?

An outline of a man's head was featured under the headline. The features were blank, with a large question mark in the center of the drawing. Under it, the words:

WHO IS HE?
WHERE IS HE?

Hearing footfalls down the corridor, she quickly folded the paper and put it aside, then peered around the corner. Edward Latting was leaving the building, using the side door next to the office, and he was carrying his black leather bag. He walked down the street, and was soon lost behind a stand of palm trees. At the same moment, Steve Gregory's pickup arrived. Parking in front of the building, he and Joe Nez exited the vehicle and entered the office.

"Joe!" she exclaimed with delight. "How good to see you! How's your grandmama doing these days?"

"Doing better, Alma," he answered. "Had to go to the hospital in Gallup last month, but she's back at the hogan now, and Aunt Jessie's having a terrible time keeping her from working too hard."

"Well, you tell both of them I can't wait till I can eat a slice of their peach pie again. When I try to make their recipe, it just never comes out right, no matter what I do."

Joe turned to Gregory. "Steve, this is Mrs. Alma Bowers, one of my family's oldest friends. Alma, this is Steve Gregory, our new police detective in town."

"We're here because we were told you wanted to see us, Mrs. Bowers," said Gregory.

"Yeah. Well, part of it was I thought they'd send Joe, and I wanted to say hello to him. But the other part is something I thought I ought to report. My tenant in thirteen: Mr. Latting. He's

sorta strange. Keeps odd hours . . . mostly goes out at night . . . says how he thinks London Bridge has a *curse* on it, how it's a 'place of evil' and should be destroyed. Those were his exact words . . . a 'place of evil.' "

"Where is Latting now?"

"He just left, a little while ago, with that black bag he always carries." Alma Bowers shook her head. "A real odd one, he is. Talks funny. Like most foreigners do."

"He's from overseas?"

"London, he said. First trip over."

"Do you have a key to his apartment?' asked Gregory.

"Sure. Got 'em to all the apartments, right here in the office. In case of emergency, you know."

She opened a drawer and took out a key. "C'mon. I'll open up thirteen for you."

The apartment was empty, as Mrs. Bowers told them it would be. Gregory walked to the framed print of London Bridge and ran his fingers along the grooves of the deep "X" scratched in the glass.

The bathroom contained no personal effects. Nez opened the closet. Bare.

"Looks as if your Mr. Latting has just checked out," said Gregory.

Office of the Chief of Police. Same day:

Anson Whitfield paced the small floor space, tight with anger. He spun around and faced Gregory, his voice sharp: *"Gone? How could he be gone?"*

"He left before we got there," said Steve. "No telling where Latting is now. We put out an APB, but so far, nothing's come in."

From behind his desk, Pete Dawson looked up at Whitfield, trying to appear pleasant. "Latting won't get far, Anson. We've got the whole county bottled up: both ends of Highway 95 . . . the airport . . . the river . . . and a Mohave County sheriff's copter is covering the desert."

"He was at Alma's all this time," fumed the mayor. "Right under your noses . . . here in town! A psycho killer. An obvious madman."

"There's no evidence that Edward Latting had anything to do with the murders," said Gregory. "Yeah, he's a weirdo . . . but that doesn't mean he's our killer."

"That's bullcrap!" snapped Whitfield. "You just don't want to admit that you let this madman slip right by you." He turned to Dawson. "Your *Chi-*

cago cop has been running this case like a damn fool."

Gregory's eyes narrowed. "I won't take any more from you, Whitfield!"

Dawson stood up. "Quit it, *both* of you."

Whitfield's jaw was set. "Detective Gregory hasn't finished his probationary period yet. He can be terminated without notice." The mayor took a sheet of paper from his coat. "This is an official request, backed by the City Council, to have Detective Steven Gregory terminated from his position. Immediately."

Whitfield tossed the paper onto Dawson's desk and stomped from the office, slamming the door behind him.

A moment of silence as Dawson scanned the document.

"Legally, this is a request," he said. "It's not an order, so I'm rejecting it." He looked hard at Gregory. "But you're walking a tightrope, Steve. A lot of important people are stirred up, and you can't afford another wrong move. Not *one* . . . or it's all over for you."

Gregory nodded. "I understand. I appreciate your keeping me on the force."

"Just walk soft," said Dawson.

As Steve Gregory moved down the hallway, Joe Nez joined him. "Heat's on, right?"

"Whitfield handed Pete Dawson an official request to have me canned. For now, I'm still on the force . . . barely. But I'm not worried about Whitfield."

"You're worried about *something.*"

"I don't buy Latting as the killer. I think we're after the wrong man."

"What makes you think so?"

"His handwriting, for one thing," said Gregory. "The registration card at Alma Bowers' place. His signature on the card doesn't match the writing on the note the killer sent to the *Herald.*"

"The note could be a phony," said Nez. "From some other weirdo who wants publicity."

"Maybe," nodded Gregory, "but I think we're missing a big piece of the puzzle. There's more involved here than a copycat killer. I just feel that there's another whole aspect to this, that we're on the wrong track."

"What other track is there?"

"I don't know," said Gregory, "but I'm driving to Phoenix to check out the Arizona State University library. Maybe I'll find something that will bring us a lot closer to the truth."

by William F. Nolan

Angie Shepherd's Home on the river. An hour before dawn:

Steve Gregory pulled the Ford pickup to a stop behind Angie's white SUV. Exiting the car with a briefcase, he moved toward the front door.

Deeply asleep, the sound of the front door bell awakened Angie. She studied the fluorescent hands of the clock on her night table and frowned. Slipping a robe over her nightgown, she moved to the door and checked the view-glass.

"Steve," she said. "It's near daybreak." Sudden shock registered on her face. "Oh, my God! Is it about Lynn?"

He shook his head, no.

"Then what are you doing here?" She stared at his unshaven face. "You look awful."

"Been up all night," he told her. "Just drove back from Phoenix." He sighed. "I could use some coffee."

He followed her into the kitchen, where she filled a coffee pot with water and put it on the stove.

"Sit down, for heaven's sake, before you *fall* down," she said. "Try the couch in the living room. I'll bring in the coffee when it's done."

Steve nodded and headed for the couch. He sat down heavily, placing his briefcase beside him, scrubbing at his eyes to stay awake.

Angie came in with two big mugs of coffee. He took the one she offered and sipped it at gingerly.

"Ah . . . good and strong. Just what I need." He gestured to the sofa cushion next to him. "Sit down. We have to talk. Or, at least, *I* have to talk."

She sat down. "Okay. Talk."

He opened the briefcase and began spreading books and papers across the large coffee table in front of the couch.

"Has there been another murder?" she asked. "Is that what all this is about?"

"No. No more murders. Not yet." He shook his head. "I can't tell anyone else what I'm going to tell you . . . and you're going to think I've flipped out. But — as insane as it sounds — I believe what I'm going to say is true."

"You've got me hooked," she said.

He laid an 8x10 glossy photo next to a Xerox copy of a magazine article. "Two photographs of a boot print," he said. "What do you see?"

She studied both. "Well, it looks like they were made by the same boot. At least, there's an identical heel-and-toe pattern."

"The glossy is brand new, taken at the spot where our killer dumped the body of Elaine Phillips into the river."

"And the other?"

"It's a photo copy of a police sketch made at the scene of a Ripper killing in 1888. And, just as you say, both appear to be identical."

She looked confused. "But, I don't —"

"Then we have *this,*" he said. Steve placed a sheet of paper next to another book photo. "A Xerox copy of the note sent to Cassie Nebel by what appears to be our killer. The book photo is of a letter sent to a London newspaper after a Ripper murder in 1888."

She leaned close to the table. "The handwriting . . . it's exactly the same in both!"

Gregory's voice was firm. "That's because the same man wrote them."

"What are you saying?"

"I'm saying — God help me — that there *isn't* any copycat killer. Never was." He paused to gather courage. "The man who butchered Lia Kelley and Elaine Phillips is the *real* Ripper."

She looked at him in shock. "Steve . . . that's totally impossible."

"Which is what I keep telling myself," he said. "But look at this line from the poem he sent Cassie Nebel: 'The stone has told me there will be more.'"

"That doesn't make any sense."

"Oh, but it *does,*" Steve countered. "I'm certain that he's referring to the lost stone found in the Thames."

"But what has that stone to do with —"

Again, he interrupted her, speaking with deep conviction. "The first murder here in Havasu occurred during the twenty-four hour period in which the stone was dedicated. It's the key to everything."

"How do you mean?"

"That stone is tied directly into the killings. When it was brought back from the bottom of the Thames River, *he* came with it. Now he's here, in Havasu, in our time — and he's repeating the same historical murder pattern all over again."

"Steve . . ." Her voice was calm and certain. "Whoever this psycho is, he's not Jack the Ripper.

Not *the* Jack the Ripper. Stones don't bring dead people back to life."

"Okay, okay. Whether you believe me or not isn't important now." He reached out to grip her shoulders. "Will you at least help me?"

"To do what?"

"I've got a plan, but I need you and Joe to help." His face looked haunted. "We've got to stop him, Angie — because he's *out* there . . ." Steve hesitated, looking past the patio window, deep into the thick Arizona darkness. ". . . and he's ready to kill again."

London Bridge.
The following night:

Two armed guards patrolled the Bridge as the waters of the Colorado River lapped softly against the stone supports, tracing a liquid boundary around the deserted Tudor Village.

At the far side of the span, a dark figure emerged from the shadows. Climbing along the base, and unseen by the passing guards, he attached plastique explosive to a granite column. He moved to another part of the column and attached more plastique. Then he repeated the process a third time. Three charges successfully in place, before a guard hailed him.

"You, there!" the guard shouted, as he drew his weapon. "Stand clear, with your hands up."

The dark man, moving spider-quick, sprinted for the grassy hill near the Bridge. The guard opened fire, but the man continued running.

As he neared the top of the slope, sirens blasted the night. Outdoor floodlights suddenly illuminated the area. Police vehicles converged. Steve Gregory and Joe Nez piled out of an unmarked car, as Pete Dawson — who had been staked out in a cable TV van — joined them.

"We've flushed out our killer," said Dawson as he ran beside the two detectives.

"Possible," answered Gregory.

The fugitive sprinted for a nearby park area.

"Block the park exit!" Dawson yelled into his shoulder radio. "We have to bottle him up!"

As the police perimeter began to tighten, the dark man removed a detonator from his coat and raised it in the air.

"Once I press this button," he shouted, "London Bridge will be destroyed. The Devil rules this place of darkness. His abode of evil must be eliminated from the earth."

"Guy's totally wacked out," said Dawson. "We're gonna have to —"

At that moment, running quick and low through the shadows, Steve tackled the dark man before the detonator could be activated. As Gregory wrestled the device from his hand, the man in black suddenly snatched up a heavy tree limb.

Joe Nez shouted a warning, but too late. The tree limb smashed into Steve Gregory's head. Before he could strike a second blow, the attacker was quickly subdued by Nez and several other officers. He was handcuffed, read his Miranda rights, and led toward a patrol car.

"This is an unclean place," the dark man declared, his voice shrill. "Beware — all of you — lest you be consumed by the powers of Satan!"

Joe Nez hurried over to his partner. Blood was dripping from the wound in Steve's skull.

"An ambulance is on the way," said Nez. "Relax, Steve. Don't try to get up."

"We nail him?" Gregory asked dizzily.

"Yeah, we nailed him," replied Nez. "We've got our killer."

Gregory looked up at his partner and smiled weakly. "Don't count on it, Joe," he said.

Lake Havasu City Police Department.
Jail Section.
Night:

The dark man was huddled on a cot in one corner of the cell, legs drawn up against his chest, his head lowered in defeat.

Dawson and a bandaged Steve Gregory stood in the corridor facing the bars. "There's your Ripper, Steve," said the chief. "Not so fearsome now, eh?"

Gregory's voice was strained, the pain he was experiencing obvious. "Sorry, Pete. That's not him."

"Are you serious?" Dawson asked in disbelief.

"He's *not* the killer."

"Hell he isn't!" snarled Dawson. "Alma Bowers ID's him as Latting, the guy we've been after. And he doesn't have an alibi for the killings . . . *and* he just tried to blow up London Bridge! Plus we found newspaper clippings about the murders in Alma's dumpster, and they have Latting's prints on them. Ran a check on the guy: Arrested and released twice for assault, once when he made an attempt to burn down a church. Born and raised in Liverpool, but he spent most of the last few years in mental hospitals in the south of England. Released last year — on medication, which I assume he stopped taking. Oh, he's our boy, all right."

"Latting may be a nutcase, but that doesn't prove he killed those women."

"You told me the murders were the work of a copycat killer," said Dawson. "And you were right. Latting fits one hundred percent."

"I was wrong on the copycat angle," said Gregory.

Dawson glared at him. "If Latting didn't kill 'em, who did?"

"There never was a copycat Ripper, Pete — only the *real* one."

Dawson stared at him, dumbfounded.

"You're talking about the guy from the 1800s?"

"Yeah. That one."

"Well, he sure is active for his age. I make it he's pushing maybe 150 by now? Must take a lot of vitamins, huh?"

"I knew you'd never believe me. Didn't expect you to. But Pete . . ." Gregory's voice broke as he swayed forward. "Pete . . . we need to . . . to . . ."

Dawson gripped Steve's arm. "You okay?"

"Dizzy. A little . . . dizzy."

"You look lousy. Didn't the doc tell you to stay in bed?"

"I had to see you . . . had to *convince* you . . ." Gregory's forehead was pearled with sweat. "Pete, listen to me. Three nights from now he's going to kill again . . . just before midnight . . . on the 30th. All part of the pattern. Gotta stop him, Pete. Can't let him . . ."

Gregory fell forward, clutching at the bars of the cell to stay upright.

"Got to catch him, Pete. Got to . . ."

And Gregory slumped to the corridor floor.

Havasu Regional Medical Center.
Night:

Steve Gregory opened his eyes, the lids sliding back slowly. He blinked several times, then tried to raise himself.

"Where am I?" he mumbled.

Angie answered. "You're in the hospital. You blacked out at the jail, and the EMTs brought you here. You've been unconscious."

"Yeah, partner, you really had us worried," said

Joe Nez, who was seated in a chair next to Steve's bed. "How do you feel?"

"Like Rip Van Winkle." Steve drew in a breath. "How long have you guys been here?"

"We hardly left," said Angie. "I went home to feed the cats; but mostly, we've been here."

Steve nodded. "I had a dream . . . about both of you. We were trapped together in the village. Going to die there. Ugly nightmare."

"That blow you took was serious," said Angie.

Gregory touched his bandaged head. "How long have I been out?"

"Three days," said Joe.

Gregory pushed himself up on the pillow, shocked. *Three days!* Then this is the 30th?" His voice was edged with panic. "Dear God!"

"What's wrong, Steve?" asked Angie.

"It's tonight!" breathed Gregory. "He's going to kill again tonight!"

"Hey, the killings are over," said Joe. "We *caught* the guy, remember?"

"No. It was the wrong man. We haven't caught the Ripper."

Joe and Angie exchanged a knowing look.

She spoke gently. "I told Joe about your new theory. He agrees with me that the case has put you under a lot of pressure, and that —"

"Don't patronize me!" snapped Gregory. "I tell you, he's out there, dammit! Whether you believe me or not."

There was a strained silence in the room. Then . . .

"Angie . . . Remember . . . you promised to help me — you and Joe. With a plan I worked out. A way to catch the killer."

"Hey," said Nez gently, "there's nobody to catch."

"I'll prove there *is,*" said Gregory. "Look . . . I've got no one else I can trust, and we're out of time. We've got to act tonight." His eyes locked on theirs. "Will you help me? Both of you? *Will* you?"

Angie and Joe stared back at him.

Havasu Regional Medical Center.
Parking Lot.
September 30, 2004. The same night:

Joe and Angie argued as they sat in her SUV near the hospital's service entrance.

"We shouldn't be breaking Steve out against doctor's orders," said Joe. "If we do, we'll be acting crazier than he is."

Angie stared out the windshield, thinking. "It's

not such a big deal, is it? Playing decoy for a killer who's *already* locked up." She sighed. "C'mon, Joe. Once Steve sees that nothing is going to happen tonight, he'll be able to shake this delusion of his."

Joe shook his head. "He's in no shape to go running around chasing ghosts. Pete Dawson will have pups when he finds out about this."

"I don't care what Dawson or anybody else thinks. We're Steve's friends. I think we owe him our help. Are you with me?"

Nez capitulated. "Okay, if you're game, then so am I." He opened the driver's door. "Let's break him out."

And they moved towards the service entrance.

Lake Havasu City.
That night:

The streets were nearly empty. An occasional vehicle passed the SUV. With Angie at the wheel, Joe listened while Steve outlined his plan.

"I'm certain that the Ripper is somewhere in the Village," said Steve. "Angie — you'll be the one to flush him out. Once you've let me off at the gate, you two head for the Marina. Take *Lady* over to the Bridge and dock her there. Pretend you're having engine trouble. Joe will be hiding inside the cabin, so you'll appear to be alone."

"And you believe this will attract him?" Angie asked.

"Are you kidding? A woman in trouble. Vulnerable. Alone. He'll go for you, all right. When he does, I'll be there to nail him from the shore side. Joe can pop out of the cabin with his .38 and we'll have him in a crossfire."

"What makes you so sure he's in the Village?" Nez asked.

"The Ripper would feel at home there. It's the logical place for him to hide. He's *there.* You'll see."

"Well," said Joe, "I've always been curious about Jack the Ripper. Should be fun, meeting him in person."

"I know you both think I'm around the bend on this one," said Steve, "but tonight I'm going to prove that you're wrong. Believe me, he'll take the bait — and this is *one* kind of fishing I'm good at."

The Tudor Village.
Same night:

With its lights extinguished, the SUV rolled

quietly into the parking lot and braked in the shadows near the main gate. Gregory got out and looked around.

"I don't see the guard," he said in a near-whisper. "Probably somewhere inside. You guys go on to the Marina."

They nodded. Angie motored away into the darkness.

Gregory removed a police automatic from his coat, checked the clip, and snugged the gun into his belt. Quickly, he climbed the iron fence and dropped to the ground inside the Village. The area was utterly silent around him. Under a full moon, the trees cast spidery shadows across the cobblestones.

Gregory moved slowly, with catlike stealth, toward the dock area beyond the Bridge. There was no hurry. It would take some time for Joe and Angie to show up with the boat. His main job now was to avoid being seen.

Suddenly, Gregory stopped. Someone was standing inside one of the tall, red, glassed-in London phone booths, just past the entrance to the King's Pub.

Keeping to the shadows, Steve moved closer. It was the female gate guard. Standing motionless inside.

Gregory couldn't figure it. Obviously, the woman hadn't entered to make a call since the booth was a landscape decoration; no phone lines were hooked up to it. Just a period piece. So what *was* the guard doing in there? Despite the risk, Steve had to know.

He made a wide circle around the booth, keeping low in the shadows. Still no movement. Now he was able to peer inside. *Christ!* The guard was propped against the glass, her eyes staring out.

Her throat had been cut.

At that precise moment, just as Steve Gregory was dealing with his shock, the Ripper lunged. Like a great dark snake, scalpel raised high and glittering in the moonlight.

Steve spun around in time to deflect the downward sweep of the blade, dropping to one knee. Before he could rise, the Ripper knocked him unconscious with a single, chopping neck blow.

Now there was time for the kill, time to use the blade properly. Gregory's head was tipped back, exposing the soft skin of his throat. One clean thrust with the scalpel and —

The Ripper hesitated, startled by a sudden sound from the water. A boat was approaching, the strong beam of its deck light probing the area.

Police? A river patrol? The Ripper ducked quickly behind the tall bulk of a double-decker bus.

Angie cut *Lucky Lady*'s power, as if the engines had abruptly failed, allowing the craft to drift into the dock. She secured the bow line, then removed one of the engine covers. Her heart trip-hammered her chest; even though she didn't believe in ghosts, and considered Steve's fear of the Ripper to be a groundless absurdity, a small voice inside stubbornly continued to ask: *What if he's right?*

She smiled self-consciously at her own fears. What if Santa slides down the chimney next Christmas? What if the Easter Bunny brings me some colored eggs? Jack the Ripper, back after more than a century? Nonsense. Foolish nonsense.

But what if?

Hidden from sight in the below-decks cabin, Joe Nez vented his frustration. His voice was a muted whisper: "We gotta be nuts. I can't believe we're *doing* this!"

Angie was about to reply when she raised her head. There was a movement from the Bridge steps. A dark figure was gesturing to her, waving her forward.

"Someone's out by the Bridge," she whispered to Nez.

"The guard?"

"No, it must be Steve, but he's too far away for me to be sure. He wants me to come over there."

"Okay, go see what's up," said Nez. "I'll hold the fort."

Angie told herself that there was nothing to fear here in the late-night darkness. Once she reached Steve, this charade would be over. He'd realize that the decoy idea was a joke, that the whole situation was simply ridiculous. He'd have to admit the truth.

She reached the Bridge steps. The area was deserted. "Steve," she called softly. "Are you here?"

"*I'm* here," said a voice directly behind her. A harsh voice. *Female.*

Angie whirled around to confront a tall figure dressed completely in black, face deeply shadowed by a wide-brimmed hat, with a gleaming scalpel in hand.

Angie's muscles locked in shock. She could barely speak. "Who are you?"

"The Angel of Death," said the Ripper, as she raised the killing blade.

Suddenly, at that instant, Joe Nez came charging out of the darkness, pushing Angie to one side so he would have a clear shot. But before he could fire, the Ripper slashed down with the scalpel, disabling the detective's gun hand. Joe's .38 clattered to the pavement. Diving to retrieve it, he slipped on the cobbles. The Ripper delivered a swift, savage blow to Joe's head with a booted heel, and Nez was suddenly out of action. He lay face down, unmoving.

As she accepted the stunning fact that Joe Nez could no longer help her, and that Steve might already be dead, Angie ran for her life. Down the lonely, shadow-haunted brick-and-cobblestone street, under the tall antique gas lamps, past the clustered Tudor buildings of Old London, she ran as a deer runs in panic from the hunter.

She darted across the main square into a narrow, dimly-lit alley behind the King's Pub. Pay phone there. Call the police!

Angie picked up the receiver to dial 911 but before she could get it to her ear the dial tone ceased.

A swift, down-slicing move with the scalpel had severed the phone connection.

The Ripper was there.

Without hesitation, Angie instantly reversed direction, sprinting for the Bucket of Blood Candle Shoppe. Its rear door was ajar and Angie darted through.

Once inside, she realized why the alley door had been open: this is where the Ripper had been hiding, here in the store. Angie had unknowingly entered the lair of the beast.

She looked around desperately for a weapon, running through the store, searching, passing rows of multi-colored candles. Here: a candle owl blinked from its perch. There: a candle leopard crouched, its red-glass eyes seeming to follow her progress.

Angie reached the focal point of the shop, where the exterior of Newgate prison had been atmospherically re-created. Above the simulated iron gate, two plaster heads were mounted on spikes.

Dizzily, she stared at them in shock as the severed heads of Lia Kelley and Elaine Phillips gaped down at her.

Angie gasped in horror as her trauma-induced illusion slowly began to fade. Once again, there were only painted plaster facsimiles on the spikes.

"Realistic, aren't they?" said a graveled voice behind her.

Angie turned, helpless now. Nowhere to run. An icy calm settled upon her. Her fate was inevitable and she accepted it. The running was over. The Angel of Death had won.

"Steve said you were here — in the village," said Angie. "He was convinced that you had risen from the past, that you were Jack the Ripper."

"That is what I have been called . . . and it is how I signed my letters. To confuse people. To make them believe that a *man* committed the Whitechapel murders."

"Whitechapel? But that was —"

"In 1888," said the tall woman. "Between August 7th and November 9th, 1888. That's when I murdered Martha Tabram, Mary Ann Nichols, Annie Chapman, Elizabeth Stride, Catherine Eddowes, and Mary Jane Kelly. It was all most satisfying. Much blood. I was in complete control."

"But how —" Angie tried to form a coherent question, and couldn't.

Angie shook her head. "That was over a hundred years ago! No one can live that long!"

"I died at the hands of London police in November of 1888," said the woman. "On London Bridge. When I fell into the Thames, a stone fell with me. That stone and I rested together, at the bottom of the river, for more than a century. The Bridge stone somehow absorbed my physical essence, which allowed me to be reborn with the blood of Lia Kelley."

Angie heard the words, but her brain could not make sense of them. The woman's story had to be the disordered raving of a lunatic.

"You intend to kill me." Angie said it dully, acknowledging to herself that her statement was fact.

"No, not yet," said the tall figure. "On London Bridge, at the stroke of midnight, I shall draw your blood, but first I have something to show you. Something special. Come with me, dear girl."

Numbly, Angie allowed herself to be led out the rear of the Candle Shoppe, along the alley, to a square, concrete-block building next to the King's Pub. The Ripper swung back a heavy insulated door and a mist of frosted air escaped from the building's interior. A meat locker which served the culinary requirements of the pub.

"Inside, now," said the Ripper as she shoved Angie bodily into the structure.

The Ripper's flashlight cast a pale beam of light over rows of hooked and hanging slabs of meat, each wrapped in a covering of coarse gray canvas. The cold gripped Angie's body as she was prodded forward. They reached the last row at the far end.

"I promised to show you something special," said the Ripper. "Now I shall honor that promise."

The older woman jerked the canvas shroud away from a hanging figure.

Angie choked out a scream, hand to her mouth.

"I knew you would want to see your friend again," she said, "so I kept her fresh for you."

Swaying there on a metal meat hook, twisting slowly in the frosted air, with her throat slashed ear-to-ear, was Lynn Chandler.

London Bridge.
Near midnight:

Wrists taped behind her, Angie was forced to the center of London Bridge — to the place of the restored stone. The moon was a white ghost in the sky. Far out on the water, a night bird cried.

"The stone will receive your blood," said the Ripper. "My powers will be renewed through you. *Your* blood will allow me to return to my own century."

Angie was too numb to respond. She no longer had any hope of survival; she was simply living out the nightmare.

"The time has almost come, Angie," said the Angel of Death. "And is this not a beautiful night to die?"

The hands of the village clock, a scaled-down replica of Big Ben, were closing on midnight. When the hour tolled, the Ripper would use the scalpel.

The blade was poised at Angie's throat.

Steve Gregory sat up. His bandaged head throbbed with pain. He was dizzy. His thoughts whirled chaotically. What happened? Where was he?

Then, with a rush, his focus became clear. The Tudor Village. London Bridge. September 30th. The Ripper. And . . .

Angie! Where was Angie?

Using the phone booth as support, Steve pulled himself to his feet, swaying with the effort. He squinted his eyes, trying to clear his mottled vision as he looked toward London Bridge.

Movement! They were *there*, on the Bridge — Angie and the Ripper. Was it already too late? Could he still save her life?

Gregory pulled the automatic from his belt and staggered toward the Bridge, encountering the inert body of Joe Nez near the stone steps. Dead? No. There was a pulse, steady and regular. Joe would be okay.

Must get up the steps. Must save her. Must save Angie.

Steve began to climb. Step . . . by step . . . by step.

His legs felt rubbery and waves of dizziness swept over him, blurring his mind. But he kept on climbing.

Just as he reached the top of the span the hands of the village clock closed on midnight. The clock's mournful bell began to toll out the hour.

"It's time, Angie," said the Ripper, as the tall figure raised the blade against the light of the moon.

"Let her go!" Steve shouted, his automatic up and ready to fire.

He moved forward, to within a few feet of the pair on the Bridge.

"When the bell stops tolling," hissed the Ripper, "she will die!"

"Shoot!" Angie pleaded. "For Christ's sake, Steve, *shoot!*"

Gregory's finger locked on the trigger. In his mind's eye a thirteen-year-old boy fell into rain-swept darkness as Steve's two bullets ripped into his chest.

The bell continued to toll: eight . . . nine . . . ten . . .

"*Do it!*" Angie commanded. "*Shoot!*"

"Say good-bye to Angie," the Ripper ordered.

Steve fired.

Kept firing.

Again and again.

Until the clip was empty.

The Ripper fell back heavily against the stone parapet, still alive, but blood gouting from a dozen wounds.

With a wheezing cry, the dark figure toppled from the Bridge.

Down . . . down . . . down . . . into the waters of the Colorado River.

And this time the stone did not follow.   Ω

AUTHOR'S AFTERWORD

My surprise revelation — that the Ripper was a woman — is not so far-fetched as it may seem. Throughout the last century, many researchers have speculated that "Jack" may have been a female who possessed surgical knowledge — which would help to explain why the Ripper seemed to vanish after each attack. No one was looking for a woman.

In his book, *The Harlot Killer,* Allan Barnard ends the Introduction with these words:

William Stewart offered the thesis that the Whitechapel harlot slayer was not a man at all, but a woman . . . able to gain the confidence of her victims. . . . Proof is lacking. . . . Still, it is most interesting to consider that the police may have been on the wrong track in searching for Jack the Ripper [when] they should have been seeking Jane the Ripper.
                                          — W.F.N.

William F. Nolan began as an artist and cartoonist, but quickly switched to writing, for both the printed page and the screen.

He is perhaps best known for Logan's Run *(with George Clayton Johnson). He has also had a very long and distinguished career as a horror writer.*

We did a special Nolan issue of Weird Tales *in 1991. His most recent collections are* Have You Seen the Wind? *(Bear Manor Media) and* Ships in the Night *(Capra Press).*

If life gives you bloodsucking freaks, Just make bloodsucking freakade

I ran my fingers through your hair
I kissed you fondly on the cheek
That was moments before — Alas! —
You turned into a bloodsucking freak.

Every time I plan a vacation
To Italy, Greece, or Spain
I cancel due to the zombies
Revived by un-forcast toxic rain.

I stoll down to the Chat 'n Chew
To indulge in graham cracker pie
Accosted soon as I walk through
The door by the Brain That Wouldn't Die.

Someone is knocking at my door
At least four or five times a week
I hope it's Witnesses, salesmen —
Anything but another bloodsucking freak.

Just last night a tentacled thing
Tried to pull me down through the drain
It really is a miracle
The way I have managed to stay sane.

Giant leeches in my bathroom
And that closet skeleton's real
My girlfriend tries to eat my face
So just how am I supposed to feel?

So baby let me steal a kiss
Let's go out dancing cheek to cheek
We'll enjoy the time while it lasts
Before you turn into a bloodsucking freak.

— Nicholas Ozment

ILLUSTRATED LIMERICK

The churchyard has all gone to weed.
The tombstones are worn, hard to read.
  There's none will come near.
  They fear that they'll hear
The things that each night come to feed.

—George Barr